Sophie's World

Other books in the growing Faithgirlz!™ library

The Faithgirlz™ Bible

The Sophie Series

Sophie's Secret (Book Two)

Sophie Under Pressure (Book Three)

Sophie Steps Up (Book Four)

Sophie's First Dance (Book Five)

Sophie's Stormy Summer (Book Six)

Sophie's Friendship Fiasco (Book Seven)

Sophie and the New Girl (Book Eight)

Sophie Flakes Out (Book Nine)

Sophie Loves Jimmy (Book Ten)

Sophie's Drama (Book Eleven)

Sophie Gets Real (Book Twelve)

Nonfiction

Body Talk

Beauty Lab

Everybody Tells Me to Be Myself but I Don't Know Who I Am

Girl Politics

Check out www.faithgirlz.com

Sophie's World

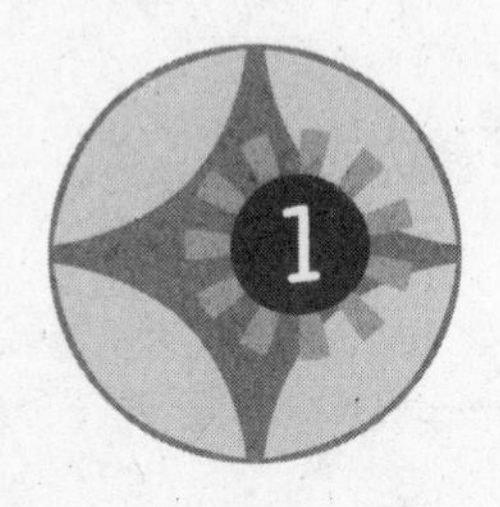

Nancy Rue

ZONDERkidz

Dedicated to the original Corn Flake Girls of Drexel Hill, Pennsylvania:

Brittany, Stephanie M., Lorraine, Jenny, Allison, Sarah, Julie, Stephanie R., Lauren, Lindsay, and Amanda.

ZONDERKIDZ

Sophie's World

Requests for information should be addressed to:

Zondervan, *Grand Rapids, Michigan 49530*

Library of Congress Cataloging-in-Publication Data

Rue, Nancy N.
Sophie's world / by Nancy Rue.
p. cm.—(Faithgirlz)
Summary: A sixth-grade field trip to Williamsburg, Virginia, stimulates the overactive imagination of future film director Sophie LaCroix, leading her to use eighteenth-century tactics to save a friend from humiliation by the popular girls.
ISBN 978-0-310-70756-1 (softcover)
[1. Friendship—Fiction. 2. Imagination—Fiction. 3. Christian life—Fiction.] I. Title.
PZ7.R88515So 2004
[Fic]—dc22 2004008751

Published in association with the literary agency of Alive Communications, Inc., 7680 Goddard Street, Suite 200, Colorado Springs, CO 80920. www.alivecommunucations.com

Interior art direction and design: Sarah Molegraaf
Cover illustrator: Steve James
Interior design and composition: Carlos Estrada and Sherri L. Hoffman

Printed in the United States of America

09 10 11 12 13 14 15 16 • 24 23 22 21 20 19 18 17 16 15 14 13 12 11 10 9 8 7 6 5 4 3 2 1

So we fix our eyes not on what is seen,
but on what is unseen.
For what is seen is temporary,
but what is unseen is eternal.

—2 Corinthians 4:18

One

Sophie—hel-lo-o! I'm speaking to you!" *I know*, thought Sophie LaCroix, *but could you please stop? I can hardly think what to do next! Here I am in a strange country—I can't seem to find my trunk, and—*

"Sophie! Answer me!"

And could you please not call me "Sophie"? I'm Antoinette—from France.

"Are you all right?"

Sophie felt hands clamp onto her elf-like shoulders, and she looked up into the frowning face of Ms. Quelling, her sixth-grade social studies teacher. Sophie blinked her M&M-shaped eyes behind her glasses and sent the imaginary Antoinette scurrying back into her mind-world.

"Are you all right?" Ms. Quelling said again.

"Yes, ma'am," Sophie said.

"Then why didn't you answer me? I thought you were going into a coma, child." Ms. Quelling gave a too-big sigh. "Why do I even plan field trips?"

Sophie wasn't sure whether to answer that or not. She had only been in Ms. Quelling's class a month. In fact, she'd only been in Great Marsh Elementary School for a month.

"So answer my question," Ms. Quelling said. "Do you or don't you have a buddy in your group?"

"No, ma'am," Sophie said. She wasn't quite sure who was even *in* her field trip group.

"You're in the Patriots' Group." Ms. Quelling frowned over her clipboard, the skin between her eyebrows twisting into a backwards S. "Everybody in that group has a buddy except Maggie LaQuita—so I guess that's a no-brainer. Maggie, Sophie is your buddy. LaQuita and LaCroix, you two can be the La-La's."

Ms. Quelling rocked her head back and forth, sending her thick bronze hair bouncing off the sides of her face. She looked *very* pleased with her funny self.

But the stocky, black-haired girl who stepped up to them didn't seem to think it was the least bit hilarious. Sophie recognized Maggie from language arts class. She drilled her deep brown eyes into Ms. Quelling and then into Sophie.

Don't look at me, Sophie wanted to say out loud. *I don't want to be La-La either. I am Antoinette!*

Although, Sophie thought, *this Maggie person could fit right in. She looks like she's from a faraway kingdom, maybe Spain or some other romantic land. She can't be "Maggie" though*, Sophie decided. *She had to be Magdalena, a runaway princess.*

Magdalena glanced over her shoulder as she knelt to retrieve the leather satchel, stuffed with her most precious possessions—

"So are you getting on the bus or what?"

Maggie's voice dropped each word with a thud. She hiked her leather backpack over her shoulder and gave Sophie a push in the back that propelled tiny Sophie toward the steps.

"Sit here," Maggie said.

She shoved Sophie into a seat three rows back from the driver and fell in beside her. In front of them, the other four

Patriots fell into seats and stuffed their backpacks underneath. They twisted and turned to inspect the bus. Somebody's mother stood in the aisle with Ms. Quelling and counted heads.

"I have my six Patriots!" she sang out, smiling at their teacher. "Two boys, four girls!"

"Eddie and Colton, settle down!" Ms. Quelling said to the boys seated between the two pairs of girls. Eddie burrowed his knuckles into Colton's ball cap, and Colton grabbed the spike of sandy hair rising from Eddie's forehead.

"Dude," Maggie muttered. "I'm stuck in the loser group again."

Sophie squinted at Maggie. "I thought we were the Patriots."

"They just call us that so we won't *know* we're in the loser group."

"Oh," Sophie said.

She craned her neck to see over Colton and Eddie's heads and get a look at the other two Patriots. The girl with butter-blonde hair squirmed around in her seat to gaze longingly toward the back of the bus.

SHE hates being in the loser group too, Sophie thought. Actually she was pretty sure the girl, whose name she knew was B.J., hadn't lost anything but her usual knot of friends. She and three other girls always walked together as if they were attached with superglue.

B.J.'s lower lip stuck out like the seat of a sofa. Next to her sat a girl with a bouncy black ponytail. Ponytail Girl tugged at the back of B.J.'s T-shirt that read *Great Marsh Elementary School*—the same maroon one all of them were wearing. Sophie had selected a long skirt with daisies on it to wear with hers, as well as her hooded sweatshirt. She always felt most like Antoinette when she was wearing a hood.

B.J. leaned farther into the aisle. The only thing holding her onto the seat was the grip Ponytail Girl had on her.

"B.J., you're going to be on the floor any minute," said Chaperone Mom. "How about you scoot yourself right back up next to Kitty?"

"What?" B.J. said. She whirled around to Kitty and yanked her shirt away.

"B.J., what's the problem?" Ms. Quelling said from farther down the aisle.

B.J.'s sofa lip extended into a foldout couch. "If I could just be with my friends in the Colonists' Group—"

"And if ants could just have machine guns, we wouldn't step on them!" Ms. Quelling said.

"But they don't," Maggie said.

"Exactly." Ms. Quelling stretched her neck at B.J. over the top of the clipboard pressed to her chest. "I separated you because y'all talk too much, and you won't hear a word your guide says. You show me my best B.J., and we'll see about next time." She smiled like she and B.J. were old pals. "You can start by hiking yourself onto the seat before you break your neck."

As Ms. Quelling moved down the aisle, Chaperone Mom stepped into her place.

"Maybe you'll make some *new* friends today, B.J.," she said.

"I'll be your friend!" Kitty piped up.

B.J. glanced at her over her shoulder. "No offense or anything," she said. "But I already *have* friends."

Chaperone Mom gasped. "Now, that isn't nice!" She patted B.J. on the head and continued down the aisle.

"Busted," said Colton, wiggling his ears at B.J. Eddie let out a guffaw, and Colton punched him in the stomach.

"Boys are so lame," Maggie said. Her words placed themselves in a solid straight line, like fact blocks you couldn't possibly knock over. She looked at Sophie. "How come you hardly ever say anything?"

Sophie pulled her hood over her head, in spite of the Virginia-humid air. She wasn't sure when she could have squeezed a word into the conversation. Besides, she'd been too busy trying to figure out the possibilities.

Possibilities such as, *what does "B.J." stand for? Bambi Jo? Probably more like Bad Jerky.* B.J. looked as if she had just eaten some and was about to cough it back up.

And what about that Kitty person with the freckles? She must be Katherine, kept locked away in a tower, and she's so desperate to escape she clings to anyone she can reach. I'll save you! Rescue is my mission in life!

Antoinette tucked her long tresses beneath the hood of her dark cloak as she crept to the castle wall and gazed up at the tower.

"What are you looking at?"

Maggie's voice dropped on Sophie's daydream like a cement block. Sophie blinked at the bus ceiling above her.

"You think it's going to rain in here or what?" Maggie said. "I think you're a little strange."

"That's okay," Sophie said as she pushed back her hood. "Most people think I'm strange. My sister says I'm an alien from Planet Weird."

"Is that your real voice?" Maggie said.

Sophie didn't have a chance to tell her that, yes, the pipsqueak voice was the real thing, because the bus lurched forward and all its occupants squealed.

"Colonial Williamsburg, here we come!" Chaperone Mom shouted over the squeal-a-thon.

B.J. whirled again, her eyes fixed on the back of the bus like a jealous cat's.

Sophie turned to the window and curled her feet under her. As she watched the yellowing late September trees flip by in a blur, a heavy feeling fell over her head and shoulders, almost like a cloak — and *not* Antoinette's beautiful black velvet cape that shrouded her in soft mysterious folds from the dangers of the night.

This cloak felt like it was woven of sadness, and Sophie had been wearing it for six whole weeks, ever since her family had moved from Houston to the small town of Poquoson, Virginia.

Houston was a *huge* city with parks and museums and *big* libraries full of dream possibilities. Poquoson was mostly one street with a Farm Fresh grocery store and a Krispy Kreme Donut shop attached to a gas station, where hordes of mosquitoes flew through solid clouds of bug spray to gnaw on Sophie's legs.

The school was way different too. Here, Sophie had to change classes for every single subject, and that made it hard to keep up. It seemed as if she would just get settled into her seat in one classroom, when the bell sent her running to the next one, hauling her backpack, and leaving her work unfinished.

Of course, her new teachers had already told her — *and* her parents — that if she didn't stare out the window and daydream so much, she could get her work done before the end of class. In Houston the other students were used to her going off into daydreams. She hardly ever got teased about it there. But then her dad got promoted by NASA and moved the whole family to Virginia.

So the staring and taunting had started all over again since school started. This field trip was the first thing that even sounded like fun since they'd left Texas.

"Won't Williamsburg be amazing?" Sophie said to Maggie.

"No. Walking on the moon would be amazing. This is just historical."

Sophie sighed. "I wish it were French history. I want to learn about that. I'm into France."

Maggie pulled her chin in. "France? This is America."

"Is it?" Colton said. "Is it really? Hey, Eddie! This is America!"

"Huh?"

Colton gave him a left hook. "Maggot just said this is America. I thought we were in China, man."

"Don't call me maggot," Maggie said.

Sophie pulled her knees into a hug. Although her family hadn't had a chance to explore yet, Sophie's mother had collected brochures about the places they would go and had put Colonial Williamsburg at the top of the pile.

"They've restored one whole area so it looks just the way it was before and during the American Revolution," Mama had told her. "They say it's like stepping right back into the past."

"How long till we get there?" Sophie said. Maggie didn't answer. She whacked Colton with his own baseball cap, threw it at him, and then threatened both boys with their lives if they didn't stop calling her maggot.

"It isn't nice to hit boys," Chaperone Mom said. "It isn't nice to hit anybody."

"Why should I be nice to them?" Maggie said. "They sure aren't nice to me."

Sophie once again stared along the dense woods lining the highway and saw a sign appear, reading, "Colonial Williamsburg." It had a little green shield on it, and Sophie felt a familiar flutter in her chest. This was real! It had its own little green shield and everything.

Sophie didn't hear Chaperone Mom's answer to Maggie. She geared up her imagination for an adventure—one that didn't include maggots or lame boys or anything not "nice" at all.

Two

My name is Vic!" the skinny tour guide said. He had a smile like a slice of watermelon, and it seemed to Sophie that he ended every sentence with an exclamation point. "Follow me and stay together!"

The Patriots' Group followed Vic across the brick bridge that led away from the Williamsburg Visitors' Center. Sophie scanned the cobblestone and brick streets for a place Antoinette might appear. Maggie's foot smashed down the back of Sophie's sneaker. *I didn't think being field trip buddies meant we had to be Siamese twins*, Sophie thought. She picked up speed.

They passed along the side of a massive brick building with a curving wall and stopped in front of a tall iron gate. "This is the Governor's Palace!" Vic informed them. "Several royal governors lived here, including Governor Alexander Spotswood—not a very nice character!"

Surely there's a place for Antoinette beyond these gates, Sophie thought. She squirmed through the Patriots to get a closer view. Those high walls held who-knew-*what* amazing secrets. But with Colton and Eddie howling and B.J. repeating "What?" over and over, Sophie couldn't even FIND Antoinette.

"We'll visit the Governor's Palace at the end of your tour!" Vic said. Sophie caught up to him and gave the palace a wistful, backward glance as they walked along, right in the middle of the street.

"Where are the cars?" she said.

Vic looked down at her with the same surprised expression most adults made when they heard her speak for the first time. "Young lady," he answered, "you will find the Duke of Gloucester Street precisely as you would have in the eighteenth century!"

I love that! Sophie thought. At that very moment, a carriage rumbled past, driven by a man wearing white stockings, a coat with tails, and a three-cornered hat. Sophie closed her eyes and listened to the *clip-clop* of the horses' hooves.

Antoinette LaCroix peeked from inside the carriage, her face half hidden by the hood of her cloak. All around her colonists hurried to and fro, calling to each other in English. She could understand them, but how she longed to hear her native French.

"Hey!"

Something smacked Sophie on the top of the head. She blinked at Maggie, who was holding her map rolled up like a billy club.

"Come on," Maggie said. "You're supposed to stay with the group." She dragged Sophie forward by the wrist to where the group stood on tiptoes at a cemetery wall.

"This is Bruton Parish Church!" Vic said. "We'll visit here on our way back too!"

"Will we get to look at the graves?" Maggie said.

"Gross!" B.J. said. "Who wants to look at dead people?"

"Tombstones here date back to the 1600s!" Vic said, walking backward and beckoning the group with both hands. Sophie felt a delighted shiver.

Next they stopped in front of the courthouse. A man in a sweeping waistcoat and white silk stockings emerged through the tall wooden doors and shouted, "Nathaniel Buttonwick! Appear before the judge, or you will forfeit your recognizance!"

"What?" B.J. and Kitty said together.

Sophie didn't have any idea what *recognizance* meant either, but she loved the sound of it. Outside the courthouse two guards pushed a man's head through a hole in a wooden contraption and lowered a wooden railing over the man's wrists.

"In the stocks till sundown!" one guard shouted.

"He has to stand there until dark?" Sophie said.

"It's not real," Maggie said.

Antoinette was appalled. She had never seen such treatment, not in the gentle place from whence she came. Had it been a mistake to come to the colonies? But Antoinette shook her head until her tresses tossed against her face. She must find her mission.

Sophie wished she had a costume—like that little girl she saw across the street pushing a rolling hoop with a stick. She had on a white puffy cap and an apron-covered dress down to her ankles and white stockings that Sophie longed to feel on her own legs. A boy chased after her, trying to knock over her hoop.

I guess boys have always been annoying, Sophie thought. She caught up with Vic in time to hear that the powder magazine—an eight-sided brick building with a roof like a pointy hat—had once stored the cannons and guns and ammunition of Colonial Williamsburg's small army.

Sophie wanted to skip as they passed through an opening in the fence. A man with a big barrel chest suddenly blocked their path and bellowed, "Halt!"

"What?" B.J. and Kitty said.

"It's not real," Maggie said again, although she looked up at the giant of a man with reluctant respect in her eyes.

The man's tan shirt was the size of a pup tent, and the white scarf tied around his massive head framed a snarling face. Sophie swallowed hard.

"Fall in!" he shouted.

Colton fell to the ground, sending Eddie into a fit of boy-howls.

"That means fall into a straight line!"

The rest of them scrambled into place. The big man picked Colton up by his backpack and set him down on his feet next to Sophie.

"Hey, dude!" Colton said.

"You will call me Sergeant! Let me hear it!"

"Yes, Sergeant!" Sophie cried out.

Eddie went into convulsions of laughter. Colton said, "Yes, Sergeant," in a mousy voice.

"You—and you—fall out!" the sergeant roared.

Eddie and Colton were banished to a blue wagon full of long poles, where the sergeant told them to stay until further notice. When Chaperone Mom started to march over to them, the sergeant yelled, "You! Fall in!"

"Oh, no, I'm the chaperone!" she said.

"We need every able-bodied individual! We are no longer a small militia—we are part of the Colonial Army! If Lafayette and his troops do not arrive in time, it will be us against the Redcoats!"

Lafayette? Sophie thought. *That sounds like a French name.*

"Eyes left! Eyes front! Eyes left!" the sergeant commanded. When he said, "Pick up your arms!" the group scurried for the blue wagon and got their "guns"—long sticks almost twice as tall as Sophie. The sergeant told Eddie and Colton that he would give them one last chance, and they grabbed their sticks to line up with the rest.

"Left flank!" the sergeant cried, and he showed them how to stand their guns along their left legs. Then he taught them how to "load," how to shift from "flank" to "shoulder," how to "make ready" and "present" in one smooth motion, and to "make fire" only when he commanded. At those words, everyone screamed, "Boom!"

Antoinette had never held a weapon before in her life, but if this was what it took to fulfill her mission, then she could do it.

"Make ready!" the sergeant cried.

With her musket firmly in her hands, Antoinette dropped to her knee, waiting for the commands to present and fire.

"*You!* You there, soldier!"

Sophie looked into the sergeant's face and clung to her stick. "Yes, Sergeant?" she said.

"You're a fine soldier. You shame the whole lot of them. You can fight in my company anytime."

"Thank you, Sergeant," Sophie said.

Afterward, Sophie floated happily down the street with the Patriots. She was now a part of Colonial Williamsburg—one of its finest soldiers.

"Hey, pipsqueak," Colton said to her.

Sophie glared at him. "That's *Corporal* Pipsqueak to you, *Private.*"

"What's she talking about?" Eddie said.

"Nothing," Colton said. "She's whacked."

But right by Vic's elbow, with Maggie walking up her calves, Sophie felt anything but whacked as she made Williamsburg her own.

Inside the houses and shops, every detail swept her back across the centuries: a powdered wig on a dressing table, a quill pen in a china holder, and a four-poster bed with mosquito netting draped down its sides. *I want that in MY bedroom*, Sophie thought.

The formal English gardens with clipped hedges helped her picture Antoinette waiting among the flowers for the delivery of a secret message. And the little brick pathways covered in ivy leading down from the streets were custom-made for Antoinette's getaways.

She loved it *all*, including the sign above the jeweler's that said, "Engraving. Watch-Making. Done in the Beft Manner."

"Beft?" Sophie said.

Of course, B.J. said, "What?"

"Best," Maggie told her.

Sophie decided to start writing all of her *S*'s that way from now on. She felt certain that Lafayette, whoever he was, had made his *S*'s just like that.

When they stopped to have a picnic in the Market Square, Sophie inched close to Vic.

"Could you tell me about Lafayette?" she said.

"The Marquis de Lafayette was a young French nobleman," Vic said. "Red-headed, very short, and small-boned. He was only nineteen years old when he bought a ship and left France secretly to help the Colonists. Without him, the patriots might not have won the war, and we wouldn't be free today."

"He *bought* a whole ship?" Colton said. "He must've had cash."

"Lafayette used his wealth to help the American colonies because he believed in fairness," Vic said. "All his life he stood against anything that was more evil than good."

"So did he make it to Williamsburg in time?" Sophie said. "The sergeant said if he didn't get here with his troops, the militia would be on its own."

Vic gave her his big watermelon smile. "You were paying attention!"

"I was too!" B.J. muttered to Kitty. They gave Sophie identical narrow-eyed stares.

"So did he get here in time?" Sophie said.

"He did! But there was almost disaster."

Sophie felt the flutter in her chest. Disaster always had possibilities.

"Lafayette moved his advance units to about ten miles north of here. Someone gave him false information—that most of the British Army had already crossed the James River. So he decided to move closer to Jamestown and attack whatever enemy troops remained."

"But the whole British Army was still there!" Sophie said.

"So did the Brits waste him?" Colton said.

"No," Vic said. "He learned about the trap and marched straight to Yorktown, where the war was won."

"Who told him about the trap?" Maggie said.

But Sophie didn't listen to the answer.

From her hiding place in the Market Square, Antoinette held her breath until the British Loyalists moved on. She didn't breathe from the time she heard their secret plans until she was sure they had gone into the Raleigh Tavern. Then she gathered up her skirts and ran for the carriage house. She had to reach the Marquis de Lafayette with the news—before he marched right into the British trap.

"Hey! Sophie!"

"*What?*" Sophie said.

She shook off the hand that Maggie had wrapped around her backpack strap.

"Fine," Maggie said. Her eyes narrowed into fudge-colored slits. "I won't tell you that everybody else is going shopping." She put up her hands. "You're way too high-maintenance."

As she stomped away, Sophie squinted at the rest of the Patriots gathered under a canvas souvenir shelter, pawing through toy muskets and Revolutionary flags. Sophie saw B.J. put something white on her head and make a face at Kitty.

That's one of those puffy caps! Sophie thought. She raced toward the tent. She ran her fingers along the three-cornered hats and white stockings and full dresses with aprons. Those, she discovered, were way too expensive, so she settled for a white cap in a bin that said "Mobcaps."

"Are you actually going to *buy* one of those?" B.J. asked.

"B.J., be nice," Chaperone Mom said. "She just wants a souvenir, don't you, honey?"

Sophie shook her head. "No. I want it for a game I'm going to act out."

B.J. stared with her mouth open as if Sophie had just announced she was having plastic surgery. Sophie knew that look, and she could almost hear her thirteen-year-old sister Lacie in her head:

Sophie, you can play your little games. Just don't tell *anyone you're doing it. Keep it to yourself or they'll think you're totally from Planet Weird.*

Sure enough, B.J. exchanged raised-eyebrow looks with Kitty.

"All right, Patriots!" Vic called out. "Complete your purchases and let's go!"

Sophie paid for a ballpoint quill pen and her cap. She tucked the pen carefully into her backpack and placed the cap on her head. Then she followed the group toward the Capitol Building. This time Sophie didn't hurry to catch up with Vic, because Kitty and B.J. flanked him, and Maggie hadn't returned to drag her along. Sophie felt the cloak of sadness descend on her shoulders.

But I haven't the time to feel sorry for myself, Antoinette thought. *I must get word to Lafayette. The fate of the militia is at stake! Glancing over both shoulders to make sure the British were nowhere in sight, Antoinette straightened her white lacy cap. She hurried down a set of stone steps and ran between the shops. It would be best to stay out of sight just in case they suspected her.*

Behind her the sound of horse-drawn carriages faded, and she hurried through a maze of hedges in a garden behind the hat shop, and then she hoisted herself over a brick wall. Antoinette stopped to catch her breath. This is a graveyard! She put her hand over her mouth.

And so did Sophie.

Sophie scanned the rows of tombstones. The rest of the Patriots were nowhere in sight.

Three

"Oh no," Sophie said to the nearest gravestone. "I'm lost."

Usually the idea of being lost had great possibilities. But right now, Sophie's heart pounded. Ms. Quelling would make the eyebrow face. Mama would say, "I'm so disappointed." And Daddy—

Sophie squeezed her eyes shut. *I have to find a way to get found!* Straightening her mobcap, Sophie ran along a dirt path through the tombstones to a large brick building. The front door opened, and a man in a necktie led a group of grownups down the steps. Sophie hung back as the man began to speak. "Please take the time to look around the church cemetery," he said. "You'll find markers dating back to the early seventeenth century."

Oh, this is that church! Sophie thought. She remembered that the Patriots' Group would have to pass this way to see the Governor's Palace. *I'll just wait for them here*, she decided. *I hope Chaperone Mom doesn't start yelling about how not nice I am, right here in the cemetery.*

"Welcome to Bruton Parish Church, ladies and gentlemen," said Necktie Man to a new group near the steps. "We ask you to please keep your voices low in the church, as this is an active place of worship and there may be people praying inside."

Sophie hitched up her backpack and hurried to join them. Chaperone Mom might yell out *here*, but Mr. Necktie wouldn't let her raise her voice in *there*.

When she stepped inside, the church itself seemed to whisper, "Shhh!"

At the end of each church pew stood a small door, so that the pews formed long narrow cubicles. Sophie slipped inside one and closed its door as Mr. Necktie filed past with his tour.

I'll hide here until I hear Vic, she decided. *If Maggie hasn't informed on me yet, I can just sneak right back into the group, and it'll be just fine.* She let out a long, slow breath and looked up at the pulpit where the minister probably preached his sermons. It looked like it was suspended in midair. *That looks high enough for Jesus to preach from*, Sophie thought.

Sometimes in church when sermons got boring, Sophie liked to imagine that Jesus himself was talking. She knew stories from Sunday school, and she'd heard people talking about what Jesus would do, so she could imagine him saying some words. But the *picture* she held of him in her mind felt *very* clear.

His kind eyes never narrowed into slits or rolled into his head like he thought she was whacked. He had a real smile too, one that couldn't switch into a curled-up lip. His whole face understood what it was like to imagine amazing things and act them out, even when every *other* girl in the galaxy was acting like she was poison ivy.

"Jesus," she whispered. "I don't think you'd yell at me just because I got wrapped up with Antoinette and got lost. I think you'd understand me." She sighed. "But Jesus—it would *really* help if I had just one friend *here* who understood me too, and we could imagine stuff together, and I wouldn't feel so lonely all the time. Do you think I could have that, please?"

She looked up at the pulpit again. *Don't be up there*, she prayed. *I wish you were here next to me and I wasn't in trouble and you wouldn't let them be mad at me.*

Someone cleared his throat and Mr. Necktie peered over her pew door. Only then did Sophie realize she was actually on her knees. "Miss, I didn't want to disturb your prayer—"

But the pew door flew open with a bang, and Ms. Quelling said in a louder-than-prayer voice, "*You* have some explaining to do."

Sophie wondered why Ms. Quelling always asked for an explanation, because she never gave her a chance to give one. Even though Sophie had to sit next to her in the front seat of the bus all the way back to Poquoson, the teacher obviously wanted Sophie to keep her explanations to herself.

And when they got off the bus, Ms. Quelling gave Sophie's mother her *own* version of the story, as if Sophie had spent the entire trip planning how to ruin everybody's day.

"It wasn't like that, Mama," Sophie said as they left the school in the Suburban.

"I know it wasn't," Mama said. "I think she's just a little upset." She looked at Sophie with her brown-like-Sophie's eyes. "And I can imagine she was terrified that something had happened to you." Mama tilted her head in that elf-like way she had, her frosty curls slipping to the side. "Soph, I know you didn't do it on purpose, but we have to make sure this doesn't happen again."

When they pulled into the driveway of their two-story gray house, Sophie's older sister, Lacie, was kicking a soccer ball to five-year-old Zeke in the front yard. Lacie and Zeke ran to the car. Neither of them had Sophie's soft voice.

"Mama, can we have the cookies now?" Zeke said.

Lacie stared at Sophie. "What's that thing on your head?" she said.

Sophie ignored them, ran into the house, and flew up the shiny wooden stairs that turned a corner on their way. She hurled herself into her room, closed the door behind her, and tossed her backpack aside.

Circling the bed, she flicked on her table lamp with the princess base and leaned against the white bookcase by the window that looked into the arms of an oak tree. Sophie wrapped her fingers around the gauzy curtains and shut her eyes.

Antoinette pulled the mosquito netting around her shoulders. She knew it wouldn't hide her from Governor Spotswood when he came thundering through the library door, but for now she must order her mind. How can I explain to him why I was dashing off into the woods? I can't tell him that I was helping Lafayette! The governor is a Loyalist. They'll put me in the stocks. Or worse—

There was an impatient knock. *Before Antoinette could say, "Come in," the library door flew open.*

Sophie peeked one eye between the gauzy curtains as Daddy came through the door. He looked taller and more big-shouldered than ever.

"Come in, sir," Sophie said.

"Sir?" Daddy said. For a second a twinkle shot through one of his blue eyes.

"In Williamsburg, we had to call the sergeant 'sir'— "

The twinkle disappeared.

"I guess Mama told you what happened," Sophie said.

"She did." Daddy pulled up the pink vanity stool and sat carefully on it. "What were you thinking, Soph?"

"I was thinking about a story I was making up," Sophie said. "And then all of a sudden, my group was gone. I guess I got carried away."

He blinked and ran his hand through his thick black hair. "At least you're honest."

I hope that counts when you start thinking up my punishment, Sophie thought.

"But you give me the same reason every time something like this happens."

"I couldn't help it," Sophie said. "You should see that place. Everything is exactly like it was back in the olden days—*exactly*!"

"They make it that way so you can learn your history—not so you can get so caught up in the fantasy of it that you wander off. Can you promise me that this won't happen again?"

Sophie thought about it, and then she shook her head.

"Why not?"

"Because—it just happens."

"And is it the same thing that 'just happens' when you stare into space in the classroom and don't get your work done?"

"Yes, sir."

Daddy's eyebrows pinched together. "Then we have to find a way to make it stop happening," he said.

There was a light tap on the door and Mama slipped in. She perched on the edge of Sophie's bed, her feet dangling above the floor.

"We're just talking about how we're going to stop all this daydreaming," Daddy said.

You *were just talking about it*, Sophie thought. *I don't* want *to stop daydreaming.*

"I guess we're going to have to go with what we talked about," he said.

What is this? Sophie thought. *Are they going to put me in the stocks or what?*

"Okay," Daddy said to her. "As soon as we can get you in, you're going to start seeing a counselor. Your mother will fill you in on all the details."

Sophie thought her eyes were going to pop out of her head. "A counselor?" she said. "You mean, like a psychiatrist?"

"No!" Mama said. "He's a counselor you can talk to." She reached across and touched Sophie's cheek. "We know you're unhappy, Dream Girl."

"And he helps kids straighten out so they can do better in school." Daddy sat up straight. "And you *have* to promise, Sophie, that you will try to do everything he says. Am I clear?"

"Yes, sir," Sophie said.

When her parents had closed the door behind them, Sophie flounced across her pillows, hair streaming.

"Please," Antoinette cried to the governor. "Please don't send me to that awful place. I'm not crazy! I have a mission to accomplish!"

"Are you nuts?"

Sophie looked up miserably at Lacie, whose compact frame stood in the doorway, still in her soccer clothes.

"They think I am," Sophie said. "And don't you know how to knock?" She flung both arms out to her sides.

"Okay, lose the drama." Lacie scooped her dark-like-Daddy's hair into a ponytail holder she'd been wearing on her wrist. "Do you *want* to go see this shrink?"

"No! He's just gonna tell me I'm weird like everybody else does, and my grades are still going to be bad, and Daddy will ground me forever, and then I'll have to sit here like I'm in prison— "

"Not that you wouldn't actually enjoy the drama." Lacie's face took on the sharp look that made her freckles fold into stern little dashes. "You want some advice?"

Like I could stop you, Sophie wanted to say.

"You need something to do," Lacie said. "So you won't even think about daydreaming."

"I don't want to play soccer, if that's what you're going to say."

"It doesn't have to be soccer. It can be volleyball or softball—"

"I'm not good at sports."

"Okay, so chess—no, not chess. That's for brainy kids."

"I'm not stupid!"

"I'm not either. I make straight A's—remember?"

Sophie sniffed. *As if you* or *Daddy ever let me forget it.*

"It's cool to make good grades if you handle it right," Lacie said. "You're smart enough if you'll just focus. You don't focus because you're off on Planet Weird, so you need something that you can think about—something in the real world."

That's just it, Sophie thought. *Sometimes I don't even like the real world.*

"You only *think* you're not good at sports," Lacie said. "Let me work with you on some basic skills."

"N.O.!"

Lacie scrunched up one eye and put her finger in her ear. "Okay, okay! Why do you have to do that? You about pierced my eardrum. A simple 'no' would do."

"Would it get you out of my room?" Sophie said.

"Probably."

"Then—simply *no*."

"All right. Fine." Lacie folded her arms across her chest the way Daddy did. "I'm just trying to help you so you won't become a total loser. Just promise me you aren't going to wear that stupid white cap to school."

"I thought you said a simple 'no' would get you out of my room."

"I'm going. I'm just telling you—"

Sophie readied for another high-pitched squeal. Lacie raced out the door.

Antoinette sighed under the mosquito netting. If it weren't for her mission to save Lafayette, she would fire Lacette, that saucy little maidservant. Then she would flee this miserable place. She would board a ship and sail triumphantly back to Paris, where they understood her for the hero she really was.

The next morning in language arts, Maggie passed Sophie a note that said, "So did you get busted?" Sophie wrote back with her quill pen: *Yef. Bufted.*

Sophie counted every minute, trying to ignore Maggie and B.J. and her group who couldn't seem to talk about anything else BUT the incident on the field trip. In social studies, Ms. Quelling took her aside and said, "You can't hope for better than a C in citizenship after your stunt yesterday. Keep your mind on your work, and STOP making your *S*'s like *F*'s."

The misery went on for days. Every day, Sophie stopped at the cafeteria door just long enough to throw away her sandwich, and then she fled outside to meet Antoinette. About a week after the field trip, on a lonely Tuesday, she was on the top of the rusted monkey bars nobody ever used.

Antoinette didn't care about rust—or the stocks—or the advancing British soldiers. All she cared about was getting to Lafayette. His encampment lay just over the hill. She knew the troops were making ready to cross the James River, right into the trap. Antoinette let her cloak fly out behind her as she grappled up the hill, ignoring the biting wind, fearless now of even Governor Spotswood himself. If she could just reach the top before—

"Hey—where are you?"

Sophie had to twist to look under her own arm. A pair of wonderful gray eyes, set in a golden face, looked up at her. The girl tucked a strand of chocolate brown hair behind her ear, where it crept out again.

"Are you climbing a hill or a wall?" she said. Sophie had never seen the girl before, and she didn't dare believe her ears.

"Hill," she said finally.

"Who are you?" the girl said.

"Sophie LaCroix."

"I know that. I mean, who are you right now?"

"I'm Antoinette," Sophie said.

She waited for the eye roll, the curled lip, the "You are weird!"

"Oh," the girl said. "So—can I play?" Her eyes took on a dreamy glow. "I could be Henriette."

Four

Sophie stared with her mouth wide open as "Henriette" climbed to the bar below her.

"Are we French?" the girl whispered.

Sophie nodded.

"Bonjour!" the girl cried.

Sophie answered, *"Bonjour!"*

"Merci, Mademoiselle Antoinette. Why are we climbing this hill?"

Sophie sucked in her breath. Her answer might send "Henriette" racing across the playground yelling "Weirdo alert!" Sophie let out the breath.

"I must get a message to Lafayette," she said. "Or else he and his troops will walk into a trap— "

"You can't go alone! It's too dangerous! I'll keep watch for you."

Sophie squinted at her through her glasses. "Can you be trusted?"

"You have my word," said "Henriette" solemnly. "I can give you no greater guarantee than that."

Sophie fought back a smile of relief and nodded seriously, whispering, "All right, then. But stay low."

Behind them, Great Marsh Elementary School transformed into the maze of gardens and stone walls of Williamsburg, and the shouts of other students became those of the British, foiled in their attempt to trick the brave Marquis de Lafayette.

The Marquis bowed on one knee to kiss their hands.

"You brave damsels must allow me to repay you in some way."

"It is enough to know we have helped you," Antoinette said, her head bowed.

"Oui, monsieur," said Henriette.

"What are y'all doing up there?"

Sophie unfolded from her bow. Four faces stared up at them.

"This is what she was doing in Williamsburg, Julia," said B.J. "Being weird." She pointed at Sophie and nudged the tall girl.

Julia tucked in her chin. Her thick, russet ponytail fell forward. "*What* are y'all *doing*?" she said again.

"Imagining," said "Henriette." "What are *y'all* doing?"

A nervous-eyed girl with short, black hair let out a squeal that reminded Sophie of a toy poodle.

"We're being normal," Julia said. She glanced at her friends expectantly, and they all nodded. The giggly one cackled with B.J. and a fourth girl, who was so thin that Sophie felt certain she'd fall over if someone breathed on her. Skinny Girl ended with a loud, juicy sniff.

"Would you like a *serviette*?" said "Henriette."

Julia flipped an impatient hand through the air. "This is just way too weird."

She turned and strode off, ponytail swishing importantly from side to side. The other three followed her like ducks.

"I have two questions," Sophie said when they were gone.

"Number one," said "Henriette," holding up a finger.

"What's a *serviette*?"

"It's French for 'napkin.' She totally needed to blow her nose, but I don't know the word for Kleenex." She held up a second finger. "Number two?"

"What's your this-world name?"

"Fiona Bunting. Today's my first day."

Sophie swung down from the bars and dropped to the ground with Fiona right behind her.

"How did you know my name already, then?" Sophie said.

"I heard B.J. talking about you in class, so I asked her your name." Fiona rolled her wonderful gray eyes. "She said it was Soapy, and then she was all laughing. That's because she's a Pop—you know, a popular girl. They think every corny word out of their mouths is funny."

Sophie gave her a sideways glance. "You didn't think it was funny—what B.J. said?"

"No! I thought it was absolutely heinous."

"Heinous?" Sophie said.

"Dreadful. Wretched," said Fiona. "Heinous *far* exceeds horrible."

"Oh," said Sophie. "I understand you."

"Yeah," Fiona said, "and I understand you too."

For the rest of the week, Sophie and Fiona lived together in the world of Antoinette and Henriette. After lunch, after school—even on the phone after supper and almost all weekend—until Lacie complained to Daddy that Sophie was hogging the line. Mostly, for Sophie, it was about what Fiona called the deliciousness of it all. Some of it, though, helped her NOT to think about going to see the counselor on Monday.

During after-lunch free time that day, Sophie and Fiona were near the monkey bars. Sophie crouched on the ground beside Fiona, holding her hand and stroking her forehead.

"*Now* what are y'all doing?"

Sophie tried to ignore the sound of Julia's voice. Henriette had scarlet fever—this was no time for conversation.

"Hello? Anybody home?"

Sophie finally looked up at her least favorite faces on the playground.

Fiona groaned, "Must you be so imperious, Julia?"

"What?" B.J. said. Kitty hovered around B.J. like a moth, echoing "What?" and sending the giggly girl into poodle shrieks.

"Willoughby—Kitty—shut *up*," Julia said.

"We're playing a game," Fiona said.

"I *know* that," Julia said.

Fiona blinked her gray eyes. "Then why did you ask?"

"Well," Julia said, "because you're lying on the ground and Soapy is patting your head like you're a cocker spaniel."

That sent Willoughby into a fresh batch of giggles.

"Willoughby!" Julia said, snapping her red braid like a whip. "I told you to shut *up*!"

"I can't help it," Willoughby said. "Her voice makes me laugh."

"Yours doesn't make *me* laugh," Julia said.

Willoughby whimpered and hid behind the shoulder of the skinny blonde.

"You should get up off the ground, Fiona," the skinny girl said. Her voice was thick, as if she still had nose problems.

"Tell me why, Anne-Stuart," Fiona said to the skinny girl. "Is there a *rule* against lying down outside?"

"There ought to be," Julia said. "There ought to be a rule against being weird, period."

"But who says what's weird and what's not?" Fiona said.

Sophie gaped at her friend. Fiona sure enjoyed an argument. Sophie usually just shrugged and went back into her daydreams when stuff like this happened. They only had about five more minutes of free time to bring Henriette back to health, and she didn't want to waste it on the Pops.

"Everybody knows it's weird to still be playing make believe in the *sixth grade*," B.J. said. "That's like a rule itself."

"Everybody knows it," Kitty chimed in. "I even know it."

"That's why everybody thinks you're strange, Sophie," Anne-Stuart said. "If you acted, you know, like normal, you'd have more friends."

Fiona propped herself up on her elbows. "Would *you* be our friend, Anne-Stuart?"

"I am so over this," Julia said, and led her train of Pops away.

Fiona lifted her face closer to Sophie's. "I didn't *think* she wanted us in her little group."

"Whatever," Sophie said. She flopped back onto her elbows. She could feel herself scowling.

"Are you mad at me?" Fiona said.

"No," Sophie said. "I just wish I didn't have to go where I have to go this afternoon."

"Orthodontist?"

"No." Sophie pulled a strand of her hair under her nose like a moustache. "Do you promise you won't tell another single solitary person about this? Not now or ever."

Fiona's eyes went round. "I promise on Henriette's soul," she said. "What's up?"

"I have to go see a psychiatrist," Sophie whispered.

Fiona sat straight up. "No way! My parents tried that on me too."

"Then—what do you think he's going to be like? I can't even imagine it—and I can imagine just about anything!"

Fiona rolled onto her belly and rested her chin in her hands. "He'll be old and bald and definitely crazier than you, but don't worry. Even though it's heinous at first, it won't last long."

"It won't?" Sophie said.

"No." Fiona looked wise. "See, the thing with psychiatrists is that if they're going to change you, you have to *want* to change. Both my therapists told me that first thing. When I told them I didn't want to change, they told my parents they couldn't do anything for me."

Sophie sagged. "I can't do that. I promised my father that I would try to do everything the counselor told me."

Fiona gave an elaborate sigh and fell back into Henriette's deathbed.

"Then I suppose our fun is over," she said. She flung her arm across her forehead.

"No, Henriette!" Antoinette cried. "Nothing will ever come between us. Not the British! Not that evil doctor! Nothing!"

Nothing except the bell.

"Don't let them change you," Fiona said as they jogged toward the building. "Don't let them."

That afternoon, Sophie trudged toward the old Suburban with her sadness cloak so heavy that she could barely lift herself into the front seat.

From the back, Zeke shouted, "Hey, Mama!" Her little brother always yelled as though he stood at the opposite end of a soccer field.

Sophie turned to look at him. His dark, thick hair stood in spikes, and his eyebrows wobbled up and down.

"You know what about Spider-Man?"

While Mama cooed over something Zeke had told her about a hundred and three times, Sophie stared glumly out the window.

I don't get it, she thought. *Zeke thinks Spider-Man* is real. *He thinks he IS Spider-Man or Peter Parker or whoever and nobody sends* him *off to a psychiatrist. I know Antoinette is only in my mind, but everybody thinks I'm a nut case. And now I have to go try to explain that to some stranger.*

She sighed all the way from the hollow in her stomach. This was heinous. Absolutely heinous.

Five

The counselor was waiting when Mama, Zeke, and Sophie arrived. He wasn't what Sophie and Fiona had dreamed up—at *all*—with his short, gelled hair and his twinkly blue eyes behind rimless glasses. He didn't look even a little bit crazy.

"Hey, Sophie," he said, reaching to shake her hand. "I'm Peter Topping, but you can call me Dr. Peter if you want."

Zeke was obviously impressed, because he immediately launched into babble about the ice cream he was about to get if Sophie didn't cry while she was at the doctor. *Too bad he wasn't the one who had to stay,* Sophie thought.

"It's okay if she cries in *this* office," Dr. Peter said. "But I'll do my best not to *make* her cry."

But after Mama assured Sophie that she *and* Daddy would be back to get her, Sophie was sure she *would* start to cry the minute she followed Dr. Peter into a bright room.

"How about we sit over here?" Dr. Peter pointed to a long window seat in the corner.

"Yes, sir," Sophie said. She hiked herself up onto some plump cushions shaped like faces and folded her hands in her lap. Dr. Peter sat on the other end.

Just as he started to open his mouth, Sophie said, "Could I go first?"

"O—kay," he said, dragging out the O. "Sure—go for it."

She took in a huge breath. "I don't really want to change, so I don't know if you can help me. I told my dad that I would try to do whatever you told me, so I'm going to—but I don't want to. I just thought you should know that."

Dr. Peter didn't laugh. Nor did he throw up his hands and say, "Then there's nothing I can do for you." He just nodded and said, "I appreciate your being so honest with me. My turn?"

Sophie just nodded.

"I'm not going to try to change you," Dr. Peter said. "I couldn't if I wanted to, which I don't."

Sophie could feel her eyes widening. "Does my dad know that?"

"He will when I talk to your parents later this afternoon."

"So—then—what *are* you going to do to me?"

"I'm not going to do anything *to* you," Dr. Peter said. "I'm just going to help you discover how you can live the best life possible. Fair enough?"

Sophie wasn't sure. She pulled a strand of hair under her nose.

"That doesn't sound good to you?" he said.

"Not if I have to give up dreaming up stories and pretending I'm in them."

Dr. Peter snatched up a pillow, one with a huge, hooked nose protruding from it, and looked into its puffy eyes. "Would I try to make her do *that*?" he said.

The pillow shook its head no.

"No way," Dr. Peter said. "In fact— " He turned the pillow to face Sophie. "We want to hear these stories of yours."

Sophie let the strand of hair drop. "You do?" she said.

"I do."

"Are you going to laugh at them?"

"Are they funny?"

"Not to me."

"Then I won't laugh."

"Are you going to tell me my stories aren't real?" she said. "Because I already *know* that."

"Of course you do. Anything else?"

Sophie reached for her hair again. "I guess there's one more thing."

"Bring it on."

"Are you going to tell me I'm too old to play?"

Dr. Peter gave the hook-nosed pillow a befuddled look. "When is a person *ever* too old to play?"

"For real?" Sophie said.

"Let me tell you a secret," Dr. Peter said. He lowered his voice to a loud whisper. "One of the main reasons grown-ups have so many problems is because they've forgotten how to play."

Sophie nodded soberly. "I see your point."

"Good," Dr. Peter said. "Now, let's hear about these dreams of yours."

He settled back into the pillows, hugging the hook-nosed one to his chest. Sophie crossed her legs in front of her and told Dr. Peter all about Antoinette and Henriette, and through it all, Dr. Peter nodded and sometimes even asked a question—like "Is Antoinette tall?"

"Oh, no," Sophie told him. "She's very small for her age, kind of like me. That comes in handy sometimes, when she has to hide herself—you know—for a mission."

"Of course," Dr. Peter said. "And where do you and Fiona act out your stories?"

"Well, mostly on the old playground nobody uses anymore. But when it's raining in the mornings, sometimes we sneak behind the stage curtain in the cafeteria. It's dusty and dark and huge."

"Very appropriate. So tell me, how do Antoinette's parents feel about her mission?"

"They worry about the dangerous things she does, but they're secretly very proud of her—especially her father."

"As well he should be," Dr. Peter said. He glanced at the clock. "I wish we had more time—this is fascinating. But I need to ask you one more question."

"Bring it on," Sophie said. She snuggled into the face pillows behind her. A nose peeked out from under her arm.

"Why do you think your parents are so concerned about your having these wonderful dreams and acting them out?"

Sophie whipped out a piece of hair and dragged it under her nose again. "They—mostly my dad—think I'm too old for pretend. They want me to be like Lacie—that's my sister—and play sports and join clubs and make straight A's. Mostly it's about school."

"What about school?"

"I don't get my work done. And I don't always hear what the teachers are saying because I'm daydreaming."

"You sure are an honest client."

"I'm a client?" Sophie said. She liked the sound of that.

"You're my client, and I'm your advisor." He grinned at her. "And right now I'm only going to advise you to do one thing."

Here it comes, Sophie thought. She tried not to let her eyes glaze over.

"I don't want you to stop making up stories and acting them out. I'm going to talk to your parents about a different *way* for you to do that. But I want to wait to tell you until after I talk to them."

"They'll say no," Sophie said. "Daddy will, anyway."

"I think the only reason he'll say no is if he can't afford it, which is why I need to talk to him first. Do you trust me?"

"I guess I have to," she said.

Dr. Peter adjusted his glasses. "You don't *have* to do anything I advise you to do. You can make the choice."

"No, I can't. I promised my father I would try to do everything you told me to do."

"Tell you what," Dr. Peter said. "Since your father asked you to try, then you should. But you still have a choice; if it doesn't work for you, you can stop."

Sophie could feel her eyes narrowing. "Are you going to tell *him* that?"

"Definitely," Dr. Peter said.

She considered that for a moment, and then she pulled her hair under her nose again.

"Does the mustache mean you're not convinced?" Dr. Peter said.

"It means I don't think my dad is going to buy it."

"Why not?"

"Because he doesn't *get* me—not like he gets everybody else in the whole entire galaxy."

"Can you give me an example?"

Sophie didn't even have to think about it. "My little brother—you met him—Zeke?"

"Right."

"He's all into Spider-Man—he actually *believes* Spider-Man is real. My dad thinks that's hilarious—he even plays Spider-Man *with* him sometimes. But I *know* Antoinette isn't real, and my father sends me to a psychiatrist. No offense."

"None taken," Dr. Peter said, "because I'm not a psychiatrist—I'm a psychologist, which is very different. Just think of me as somebody you can talk to."

Sophie nodded.

"How about another example?"

Sophie resituated herself. "Okay—Mama. She's the most creative person in the *world*. She has her Loom Room over our garage, and she weaves fabric all by herself."

"So that's where you've inherited *your* creativity."

"But that's what I don't *get*!" Sophie said. "She uses her imagination—and Daddy is all proud of her. I use *my* imagination, and he thinks I'm too old for it!"

"You know what, Sophie?" Dr. Peter said. "There are probably some reasons for that—some of them good, some of them maybe not so good. I'm going to get right on that, though, okay?"

Sophie sat in the waiting room while Dr. Peter talked to her parents. She swung her legs and wished she knew what they were saying in there.

Madame LaCroix nodded gracefully as the great Dr. Pierre LaTopp described Antoinette's rare creative abilities. But Monsieur LaCroix sat in the corner with his arms folded across his chest and scowled. Antoinette knew what he was thinking. "Ridiculous!" But Antoinette did not despair. She knew the great doctor would make him understand. After all, Papa was proud of her. Secretly so proud.

Sophie let the dream-air puff from her lips. *I just want to be understood*, she thought. *Why can't I have that?*

Suddenly Sophie remembered thinking those words before. She had prayed the same thing in Bruton Parish Church. *Wow!* she thought with a jerk. *It happened! I have Fiona. That must be because of God!*

But what if Daddy and Mama won't let me keep Fiona after they talk to Dr. Peter because she's a dreamer like me? Sophie swung her legs harder. *What if they won't even let me keep Dr. Peter after he says he won't make me change?*

That would be heinous, she thought. *Because I think he might understand me too.*

Madame LaCroix came to her, holding out both hands, tears glistening in her eyes.

"I am so sorry, my precious daughter. How could I ever have asked you to give up your dreams?" Antoinette closed her eyes, fighting back her own sobs. Now—could she even dare to hope that Papa would feel the same way?

"You catching a nap, Soph?" her father asked.

Sophie opened her eyes to see Daddy standing over her.

"Do I get to keep Fiona as my friend?"

He looked completely confused. "Who's Fiona?"

Sophie took a deep breath. "I know Dr. Peter told you I can keep doing my stories, and you hate that, and you're going to make me stop, and Fiona won't play with me anymore, and she's the only friend I have, and if I have to give her up I'll curl up and die a miserable death."

Her dad stared. "Soph, that is the most bizarre train of logic I've ever heard. Does that actually make sense to you?"

"Darlin'," Mama said. "I'm so happy you have a friend and that she's somebody you feel comfortable with." She looked at Daddy. "We never said you couldn't play with your friends."

"As long as you don't—" But Daddy stopped when Mama nudged him with her elbow. Sophie felt her hands going clammy. She had never seen them disagree about one of the kids.

"We want to make a deal with you." Daddy put on what Sophie knew was his game face. "Dr. Topping thinks it would be a good idea for you to record your stories with a video camera. You can act them out and record them—instead of dreaming them up during class. At least that way, you're getting something practical out of it. It won't hurt to learn how to use a camera."

"You mean like a movie director?" Sophie said.

"Sure," Mama said. "I think it sounds fun."

Sophie's thoughts swirled toward her like stars in hyperspace. She put her hand up to her forehead to slow them down.

"We don't have a video camera," she said. "I don't even know how to turn one on."

"That's where the deal comes in," Daddy said. He rubbed his hands together. "I will get you a camera—and I'll show you how to use it. Then you and Viola— "

"I think it's 'Fiona,' " Mama said.

"You two can create films with it if—and this is where your part of the deal comes in— "

I knew it, Sophie thought. She held her breath.

"If, starting with your next progress report, you have at least a C for the week in every subject. I know that you can do a lot better than that— "

"But it's a start," Mama said.

"That's our offer," he said. "What do you say, Soph?"

Daddy stood there then, arms folded, while Sophie fended off the shooting stars. The video camera had *huge* possibilities. But all C's? In less than two weeks? She felt so far behind already, there was no way she could catch up. Besides—she wasn't sure she knew *how* to make good grades.

"I don't know if I can *do* that," she said. "I'll *try*— "

"You're not stupid, Soph," Daddy said. "Anybody who can remember whole scenes of dialogue from a movie can retain enough facts to pass a sixth-grade history test."

"We'll help you any way we can," Mama said.

"That's a no-brainer." Daddy chuckled. "You have a scientist living right in your house. Science and math should be a snap for you with me around."

I hate science and math, Sophie wanted to say. *I hate school, period. And it hates me!*

"I guess I can try," she said.

"You're going to have to do more than try," Daddy said. "We'll have to see all C's on the next progress report." He pretended he was hitting a golf ball.

Antoinette moaned. There was yet another obstacle. But with a tilt of her brave French chin, she stiffened her lips and spoke aloud—

"Okay. It's a deal."

Six

It was raining the next morning—Tuesday—so Sophie went straight to the secret backstage place. She—and Antoinette—were wailing inside themselves.

"Antoinette! You look vexed."

Sophie squinted through the dusty dimness to find Fiona perched on top of a pile of old stage curtains.

"Does 'vexed' mean depressed?" Sophie said, climbing up beside her.

"More like distressed beyond words."

"Then I am."

"Uh-oh. Your psychiatrist was a total weirdo, right?"

Sophie shook her head so hard she stirred up dust in little gray clouds. "No! He was brilliant. He even said I shouldn't give up making up stories and pretending them."

Fiona's eyes widened. "So what's the problem?"

"It's totally heinous," Sophie said. And then she told Fiona all about the "deal."

"We could make *amazing* films—*brilliant* films," Fiona said.

"*If* I can pull a C in everything by *seven days* from now, which *isn't* going to happen."

"Why not? It's not like you're in classes for slow kids."

"I *should* be!" Sophie could feel tears threatening, but Fiona had a gleam in her gray eyes.

"What?" Sophie said.

"I'm an experienced tutor. Did it all the time in my old school."

"You could help me?" Sophie said.

"Hello?" Fiona's heart-shaped mouth formed a pink grin. "I'm your best friend, right?"

"But the teachers aren't going to let you sit next to me and help me the whole time. Especially Ms. Quelling."

"You mean Ms. Cruelling," Fiona said. "We'll just have to figure it out."

Fiona slid down from the pile of curtains, dug around in her backpack, and climbed back up with a spiral notebook with purple sparkles on the cover.

"This is my Idea Book," she said. She pulled a matching purple gel pen out of the spirals and folded the cover back with a professional air. "You miss stuff because you daydream in class, right?"

"Right," Sophie said, sagging again.

"So when you start drifting off, I'll make a signal—like smacking the desk."

Fiona demonstrated, raising dust from the pile of curtains. Sophie coughed.

"That's it!" Fiona said. "Coughing!"

"You mean, if you see me going off, you could just, like, clear your throat— "

"Brilliant!" Fiona said. "And then if that didn't get your attention, I could go on to a dry cough, like I had something in my throat."

"And if *that* didn't do it, you like bring up a hairball!"

By the time the bell rang, they had formulated an entire code.

Sophie managed to pay attention with an occasional hack from Fiona during language arts and social studies. In computer class, Ms. Yaconovich had made Sophie sit next to her desk since the first week of school, but Ms. Y wandered around the room a lot, pulling the Pops off the Internet.

Nothing bored Sophie more than moving paragraphs around, especially with what Fiona called mundane topics, like the amount of gold there was in Fort Knox.

But no matter how mundane, Antoinette had a job to do. And if her commanding officer wanted her to spy on the treasurer to preserve the colony's gold, then she must. The treasurer could be a Loyalist, and their precious savings could wind up in British hands. She peered into the tiny Treasury window.

A shadow fell across the beam of moonlight. Pulling her cloak around her, she ducked beneath the footbridge to avoid being seen.

"Your friend's got bronchitis or something," Maggie said.

Sophie saw Fiona doubled over, face purple and hacking from her chest in loud gasps.

"Oh no!" Sophie cried, and flung herself past three computers to reach Fiona's side.

"Fiona! Are you okay?"

"Yes!" Fiona hissed through her teeth. "I was using the code! I got all the way to Level Five!"

"Oops." Sophie whispered. "My bad."

"All right," Ms. Y said in her dry-as-sand voice. "Back on task."

Sophie took in a deep breath and went back to moving paragraphs around. She managed to get the assignment done before the bell rang.

"Could that have been any more boring?" she said to Fiona in the hall.

"Okay, forget it," Fiona said. "That scene is way over." She grabbed Sophie's arm and steered her toward the cafeteria. "I just had the most brilliant idea."

"For saving the militia?" Sophie said.

"This is better. Every time a new kind of video camera comes out, my dad buys it. We have like an entire attic full of old ones that still work. I bet he would just give one to you." Her eyes danced. "And *that* means you get your dad out of your face even *sooner*."

"He will totally say no," Sophie said. "He always says no when it's me. When it's Lacie, he always says yes."

Fiona pursed her mouth into a rosebud. "Sophie, you have to stop being so pessimistic."

Sophie didn't even have to ask what *that* meant.

Antoinette rescued Henriette from a gold-filled pirate ship during free time after lunch. All through health, Sophie noticed Fiona's occasional "ahem" from her side of the room, but in math, Sophie never let her get past a Level Three bronchial spasm. By science, Fiona only had to fake pneumonia twice the whole class period. Sophie actually raised her hand to answer a question.

"That's the first day you haven't gone into a daze in my class," Mrs. Utley said after the last bell rang. She smiled as she spoke in a way that made all her soft chins wiggle. "Keep it up, Sophie, and you might actually move up to a D on your next progress report."

"Move *up* to a *D*?" Sophie wailed in the hall to Fiona. "My life is over!"

"She thinks it'll make you work harder, just to show her she's wrong."

"What if she isn't? What if I do get a D on my progress report? What if we don't get to play together ever again?"

"What if you stop thinking up that kind of stuff and concentrate on Antoinette? We have to make a movie!"

Sophie felt herself wilting. "Do you really think I can do this?"

"I don't think—I *know*," Fiona said. "I'll call you tonight, *mon amie.*" She grinned. "That means 'my friend.'"

Sophie watched Fiona flit toward a black SUV. When Fiona opened the car door, the woman in the driver's seat chattered away in a foreign language to two little heads sticking up out of boosters in the middle seats.

Fiona popped her head out the window and yelled, "Call me as soon as you talk to your dad!"

But Sophie barely had a chance to say hello to Daddy when he walked in at suppertime just as the phone rang. It was a way-excited Fiona.

"He said yes!" she shouted into Sophie's ear.

"I don't know who that is," Lacie said, "but she doesn't need a telephone. Sophie, you have to help set the table. Get the knives and forks."

Sophie cradled the phone to her neck and pulled open the silverware drawer.

"Your dad said yes?" she said.

"He said to pick out any camera you want. We'll bring some over."

Sophie shoved the phone closer to her lips. "I haven't even asked my dad yet—"

Daddy looked up from a stack of mail. "What haven't you asked me?"

"My dad wants to talk to your dad," Fiona said. Sophie put her hand over the receiver and handed it to her father. He looked as if he had no *idea* what was going on.

But as she was dropping the last fork into place, Daddy hung up the phone and said to Mama, "Super nice guy. Very intelligent."

"Who?" Mama said.

"Viola's father," said Daddy.

"Fiona!" Sophie and her mom said together.

Daddy picked up Zeke just as he was about to poke his Spider-Man action figure into the spaghetti sauce bowl. "I'm going to *buy* a video camera from him, Soph. He's coming by next Saturday, *after* you've taken your tests."

"Does she still have to get a C in everything?" Lacie said.

"Is that your business?" Mama said.

"I still think you ought to make her go out for a sport," Lacie said.

"How about we sit down and ask the blessing?" Mama said. Zeke insisted they say the prayer four times because he had just learned it. Then Lacie snapped her napkin into her lap. "So some shrink says Sophie needs a video camera and she just gets one? Failing grades and all?"

"I'd watch that tone if I were you," Daddy said.

Lacie turned to Sophie and looked ready to explode right into the pasta. "I told you not to tell any of the other kids you were seeing a shrink!"

"It's nothing to be ashamed of," Mama said.

"True," Daddy said. "Although I don't think we need to be telling everybody our family business."

"This is going to get all the way up to the middle school, isn't it?" Lacie said.

"I only told Fiona," Sophie said.

"And she told her father, which means her mother probably knows— "

"I'm not even sure her mom speaks English," Sophie said.

Mama poised the salad tongs over the bowl. "Really?"

"She was talking some other language today in their car."

"Well, her dad speaks perfect English," Daddy said. "And I'm sure he has better things to do than spread gossip about Sophie, okay?"

Antoinette put her hands over her ears. Why did these noble people even listen to that little scullery maid? All she did was make trouble. Well, it wouldn't be long before saucy Lacette realized how Antoinette rose high above all such mundane things—

"Dream Girl," Mama said. "You need to eat."

Beside her, Lacie grunted and tore a piece of garlic bread in half. Sophie felt certain it was meant to be her.

Fiona and Sophie tried to pass the week until the next Saturday by concentrating on the first scene they were going to film when Sophie got her camera. *When*, not if. Sophie worked on homework with Fiona over the phone, and Fiona checked her work every morning—just in case Antoinette had taken over.

But every day on the playground after lunch, they launched into Antoinette and Henriette's stories no matter who might be around. And each time Fiona and Sophie climbed down from the monkey bars, Maggie lurked nearby. They made a pact to find out what she was up to.

On Thursday, just before end-of-the-week tests, Fiona and Sophie caught up to Maggie on their way to math. Maggie was walking in that very straight way she had, her head moving almost like a machine as she looked from side to side.

"Hi, Maggie," Sophie said.

Maggie turned to look at them. There was no expression in her eyes.

"You were watching us play, weren't you?" Fiona said.

"Do you have a problem with that?" Maggie asked.

"No!" Sophie said. The last thing she wanted was trouble. It wouldn't look good on her progress report.

"We just wondered," Fiona said.

Maggie hesitated, and then she nodded and fell in heavily beside them as they continued down the hall. "I mostly watch the other kids watching you," she said. "They think you're weird."

"So what else is new?" Fiona said.

"We're used to it," Sophie said. This felt so much easier with Fiona by her side.

"I know you guys make up stuff and play it," Maggie said. Her words thunked like tennis balls against a wall. "I like to play games like that too. Only I would never do it where these people could see me. You're just asking for it when you play make-believe out in the open."

"We're okay with it," Fiona said.

"We're not embarrassed at all," Sophie said.

"But you hate the teasing." Maggie said. "I know you do."

"They're just clueless Pops," Fiona said.

"I'm just telling you," Maggie said.

They walked the rest of the way to Mrs. Utley's room in silence. When they got to the door, Maggie said, "I'd play with you if you did it outside school. You don't play sports, so you're free after school."

"We have to get to class," Fiona said.

They hurried to their places. Sophie watched as Maggie sat at a table on the other side of the room.

"That's creepy," Fiona said. "It's like she's spying on us all the time."

It felt that way to Sophie too. And to Antoinette—

A cold chill crept up Antoinette's spine. Why did Magdalena lurk nearby always? Could she be a spy for her country? Was she after the gold as well? Perhaps she worked for the pirates.

Antoinette glanced at Magdalena from behind her cloak. This girl would bear watching—careful watching.

"Ahem!"

Sophie looked at Fiona. "Good," she whispered. "You got it at Level One."

"Thanks," Sophie said. "What would I do without you?"

Sophie stuck out both of her pinky fingers. Fiona hesitated and then linked her own pinkies into Sophie's.

"That's our secret handshake," Sophie whispered.

On Friday morning, Fiona greeted Sophie on the stage with a frosted Pop-Tart.

"You can so do this," she said as she broke off a piece and stuck it into Sophie's mouth. "It's your mission."

Sophie felt her face soften with Antoinette thoughts.

"But don't go there," Fiona said. "Not until you get the camera. Tomorrow!"

"Progress reports don't come out till Monday," Sophie said.

"But you can find out your test grades today. Your dad's going to be so psyched; he might not wait till Monday. Come on—secret handshake."

That sealed it. Sophie marched into language arts and answered almost every question on the test. She knew the answers to all of them, but she didn't have time to fill in the last two.

"No worries," Fiona told her between classes. "You still probably got a C."

Social studies felt even easier. But when Antoinette began tickling herself with her quill pen, all Fiona had to hit was Level Two, and Sophie recovered. After their computer test, they practically danced to their chairs in the cafeteria. Maggie leaned across the table.

“Here comes Ms. Quelling,” she hissed. “Don’t look at her! She’s mad.”

“She’s always mad,” Fiona said, glancing up.

Sophie’s heart froze when Ms. Quelling riveted her eyes first on Sophie and then on Fiona.

“I want you two in my room right now,” she said. “We need to talk about *cheating*.”

They followed her down the hall and into her classroom, their clammy hands clinging to each other.

“Sit,” Ms. Quelling said. The girls sank into side-by-side chairs. Ms. Quelling picked up two papers. “How do you explain your almost identical answers on my test?” she asked, flicking her bright red nails like tiny daggers. “I thought you’d at least *dream up* an explanation.”

Somehow Sophie found her voice. “I knew the answers, and I wrote them down.”

“Suddenly you just *knew* the material after doing nothing in my class for six weeks?”

“I’ve been doing all my homework this week. And Fiona helped me study.”

“That’s right,” Fiona said. “We studied a *lot* together.” She pulled her bow-mouth into a line. “You think that’s cheating?”

“*That* isn’t cheating,” Ms. Quelling said. “And I might even believe it, if someone hadn’t reported to me that you have some kind of secret code going on.”

“We do,” Sophie said.

Ms. Quelling’s eyes went round. “So you *did* cheat?”

“No!” Sophie said. “We don’t use it to cheat. Fiona coughs at me when she sees me daydreaming.”

“Everybody wants her to stop drifting off,” Fiona said in a voice much pointier than Sophie’s. “I’m just helping her.”

Ms. Quelling laid the papers back on her desk. She looked disappointed.

"All right," she said. "I guess I don't have any choice but to believe that. I don't have any proof. But know this—I am going to be watching y'all *very* closely. Do I make myself clear?"

"Yes, ma'am," Sophie said before Fiona could say anything.

"Y'all go to class now," Ms. Quelling said. "Lunch is almost over."

Sophie bolted for the door, but Fiona lingered at the table.

"What is it?" Ms. Quelling said. Her voice stretched out like a rubber band. Fiona pointed to the test papers. "Could we please see our grades?"

Ms. Quelling made a loud click with her tongue. "They're both the same."

Fiona turned the papers over and grinned at Sophie. "B-plusses!"

"No way!" Sophie said. "I never made a B-plus my whole life!"

"Exactly my point," Ms. Quelling said. "Now go, both of you."

"I've been looking forward to seeing you again," said Dr. Peter as he ushered Sophie to their corner window seat that afternoon. "I want to hear more stories."

Sophie snatched up some hair. "I don't have any stories today. I'm sorry. If you're really disappointed, I can make up one right now."

Dr. Peter wrinkled his nose, but just a little. "I'm sure you could, but I'm curious. Why no stories today?"

"Antoinette would never have a problem like this," she said. "It's too heinous to even talk about."

Dr. Peter leaned forward. "Listen, Sophie: I will never tell anyone anything you say to me in here without your permission. What you tell me stays just between you and me."

"Would you put your hand on a Bible and say that?" Sophie said.

"I can do that," Dr. Peter said. "But I'd rather you just trust me."

Sophie squinted at him through her glasses.

"Do you even *have* a Bible in here?" she said.

"I couldn't help some of my clients if I didn't have the Bible."

"Oh," Sophie said. She took a deep breath. "Okay. Here's what happened." She told him all about Fiona and the deal with Daddy—and about Ms. Quelling and the cheating thing.

"If I have Ms. Quelling watching me every single second," Sophie told him, "and maybe the other teachers too, when she tells them—*which* she *will*—how am I supposed to focus? Already I only got a C-minus on my math test because I was so vexed!"

Dr. Peter tapped his lips with his thumbnail. "I understand you go to church and Sunday school every week."

"I do," Sophie said.

"So do I," he said. "Do you like it?"

Sophie took stock of her split ends. "Sometimes. But other times I daydream that it's Jesus up there preaching. That's okay, don't you think?"

"Absolutely," Dr. Peter said. "In fact, I was just going to suggest something along those lines."

"No, you weren't! Were you?"

"I wouldn't lie to you, Sophie," he said.

Sophie searched his face. There was no nose wrinkling or anything.

"I believe you," she said. "You seem very trustworthy."

"Here's my suggestion," Dr. Peter said. "As always, you can simply try it, and if it doesn't work, we'll try something else. But I think this is going to be perfect for you." He used his hands to explain in the air. "At home, when you're yourself and not Antoinette, I want you to picture Jesus, maybe the way you dream about him in church. And then I want you to talk to him about all these problems you're having."

"You mean out loud?" Sophie said.

"It doesn't have to be out loud. You can whisper, or you can just think it in your mind. Just be perfectly honest with him. You don't have to worry about what he thinks, because he already loves you totally. Just talk to him every day, even just for a few minutes."

"Am I supposed to imagine him answering me?" Sophie said.

Dr. Peter shook his head. "No. That's where it's different from your other daydreaming. You'll need to let him talk for himself."

Sophie could feel her eyes popping. "He's going to *answer* me? Like, out loud?"

"Probably not out loud like your father's voice or mine. Some people hear the Lord that way, but I personally don't."

"Then how?" Sophie said.

"I can't tell you exactly. You might feel something peaceful. Or you might not feel anything right away, but then later you'll realize something has changed. Sometimes Jesus gives silent answers."

Sophie pinched some of her hair between her nose and her upper lip and nodded. Dr. Peter pushed up his glasses.

"I don't think you're sold on this idea," he said. "But think about it and give it a try."

"One try?" Sophie said.

He twinkled a smile at her. "How about once a day until we meet next week?"

Sophie sighed. "All right," she said.

"One thing you can be sure of: he's going to listen."

That night as Sophie knelt by her bed to pray, she thought, *What if Lacie comes in and sees me and tells Mama and Daddy I'm playing Joan of Arc in here? What if Daddy thinks I'm double-weird? I never see* him *pray except in church and at the dinner table. What if I tell Fiona I'm doing this — and she doesn't want to be my friend anymore? I don't even know what religion she is.*

"Sophie?"

She jumped up and knocked her princess lamp against the headboard.

"You okay?" Daddy said through the door. "Sounds like the place is falling apart."

"I'm fine," Sophie said.

"Okay — lights out, then."

Sophie listened to Daddy's feet padding to Lacie's room.

"Come on in, Dad," she heard Lacie say. "Check out this game schedule."

Sophie shut her eyes. The kind face of Jesus smiled at her.

"Jesus," she whispered. "Does Daddy love Lacie more than he loves me? I should have told him and Mama about today, but I'm afraid. And Lacie always gets A's in citizenship. Lord, I don't want to feel like this. Amen."

But Sophie didn't feel peaceful. She just hoped that Dr. Peter was right.

Seven

Saturday dragged past breakfast and cartoons, past lunch and chores until the black SUV finally pulled into the driveway. Sophie hadn't had a minute alone to ask over the phone, but she hoped for the millionth time that Fiona hadn't told her parents about the cheating accusation.

But the minute she saw Fiona bolt out of the car, Sophie forgot about that.

Antoinette gathered up her skirts and rushed breathlessly to meet her friend. Although she knew it wasn't ladylike, Antoinette rushed past the woman climbing down from the carriage; so eager was she to get to Henriette.

"Whoa, there!" she said.

"Sophie—watch where you're going!" Daddy said.

"My word! Are you hurt?" said Mama.

Sophie snapped back to the real scene. A slender woman lay halfway on her back on the driveway. *That's not who picks up Fiona at school*, Sophie thought. Daddy pinched his eyebrows together as he grabbed the woman's hand.

"You need to be aware of your surroundings," he said to Sophie. "You knocked down— "

"Amy," said the woman, who rose to her feet. "Amy Bunting. And don't worry about it. I get tangled in those two almost daily." She nodded toward Fiona's little brother and sister who had climbed from the SUV and were already chasing Zeke.

A very tall man with bright eyes and narrow shoulders introduced himself as Ethan Bunting. When Fiona introduced Boppa, her grandfather, she planted a kiss on top of his bald head.

"Fiona talks about you all the time," he said to Sophie.

"Boppa, would you mind—?" said Mrs. Bunting. Boppa gave a here-we-go-again smile and headed toward the porch where Fiona's little brother and sister were climbing the railing with Zeke right behind them.

"I thought that other lady was your mom," Sophie whispered to Fiona.

"Marissa? No, she's our new nanny. Boppa loves to joke about how long she'll last. We've never had one stay longer than six months."

"How come your mom didn't go after them?" Sophie asked Fiona.

"She can save your life on an operating table, but she can't make those kids do anything. They're brats."

"Your mom's a doctor?"

"Yeah. She's a thoracic surgeon."

Sophie didn't ask her what *that* meant, but it sounded important and probably messy. Their dads stood at the back of the SUV, examining cameras. Fiona grabbed Sophie's hand and squeezed it as she dragged Sophie over there.

Daddy stood up straight just then, and Sophie's chest fluttered. He was holding a video camera.

"Is that it?" Fiona asked. "Is that the one?"

Daddy nodded, still peering at the camera with the earpiece of his sunglasses in his mouth.

"Yes!" Fiona said. "Can we play with it now?" She reached to snag the camera.

She's going to get in so *much trouble*, Sophie thought.

But Mr. Bunting just said dryly, "You're so ladylike, Fiona." Daddy held the video camera out of Fiona's reach, his eyes glued to Sophie's.

"We saw our grades already," Fiona said. "She did great. Are you gonna make her wait till Monday?"

"Sophie knows when she can have the camera," he said, still staring straight into Sophie's eyes. "The Buntings have to leave shortly. They're on their way to Richmond for the weekend. I'll just hang onto it until we see that progress report Monday morning."

"Don't worry," Fiona whispered as her family loaded back into the car. "You *know* you're going to get it."

Antoinette did not appear for the rest of the weekend. But on Sunday night, Sophie grabbed her mobcap and stuck it on her head. She closed her eyes and tried to imagine Jesus.

"Is it ever going to be okay here?" she asked him. "Ever?"

Eight

As Sophie walked into school on Monday morning, she felt like throwing up her oatmeal. She imagined taking her progress report from class to class, her fate flowing from the tips of her teachers' pens as each signed off the form.

Antoinette pressed her hand to her stomach and tried not to think about the wretched gruel she'd eaten at the empty farmhouse. Lafayette's encampment lay before her, and she must now cross the James River without becoming seasick.

"Don't worry," Fiona said as they sat down in language arts. "We'll get seat work today so the teachers can fill out the progress reports—"

Anne-Stuart leaned across the table. "So, how do you think you'll do in here?" Willoughby leaned over Anne-Stuart's shoulder with a smile. They wore identical shirts.

"Are you talking to *me*?" Sophie said.

"I just wondered how you think you'll do on your progress report."

"I got a C on the test," Sophie said. "I didn't get to finish all the questions."

"Really?" Anne-Stuart said. She cocked her head, her headband stretching her hair smoothly back from her forehead. "I thought you would do really well."

"You did?" Sophie said.

"You had plenty of help," Anne-Stuart said. "What did you get, Fiona?"

"A-minus." Fiona's nostrils flared like little trumpets.

"We studied together," Sophie said.

Anne-Stuart put a Kleenex to her mouth and coughed. Behind her, Willoughby coughed twice, and then yelped like a terrier.

"I don't get it," Anne-Stuart said to Fiona. She sniffed several times, and Sophie wondered why she didn't use the Kleenex for her *nose*. "How come Sophie got a C and you got an A-minus?"

"I don't know," Fiona said through her teeth.

Anne-Stuart coughed again into the Kleenex. Then Willoughby hacked like a cigarette smoker. Across the room came the sound of someone coughing up a lung. Sophie saw B.J. staring straight at her. Kitty cackled nearby, her ponytail flopping like a flounder.

Anne-Stuart stopped choking and leaned toward Sophie. "I guess a C is pretty good for you, huh?"

"Yes," Sophie said. "I'm trying to improve."

"Not that it's any of *your* business," Fiona said.

Anne-Stuart gave an innocent blink, her eyes sinus-watery, and coughed into her Kleenex. Willoughby choked and yelped as the last bell rang.

"All right, people," Mr. Denton said, his voice like a dial-tone. "I see only one person ready to work."

Sophie looked where he was pointing with his chin and saw Julia glance up from her open literature book as if she were surprised by the attention.

"She is so corny," Fiona whispered to Sophie.

Sophie pulled up the hood on her sweatshirt and stared at her open literature book without seeing a word.

At the end of the period, Mr. Denton laid the progress report in front of Sophie with a smile. There was a firm black C on it and the comment: *Much improvement! Sophie seems to be adjusting now.*

"We're on a roll!" Fiona said in the hallway. Sophie linked her arms in hers all the way into Ms. Quelling's room.

"I'm moving you, Sophie," Ms. Quelling said before Sophie could put down her backpack. "Over here where I *know* no one is going to help you." Ms. Quelling pointed to a seat right next to Julia and across from Anne-Stuart and Maggie.

"I trust y'all," Ms. Quelling said to them.

Julia and Anne-Stuart nodded solemnly at the teacher. Maggie offered one of her open stares, but the other girls didn't glance her way.

"That way you won't be tempted to even look at Fiona," said Ms. Quelling. "The assignment is on the board."

Anne-Stuart and Julia flipped their textbooks open.

"Aren't you going to get started?" Maggie said to Sophie.

Sophie tried to read about the writing of the Constitution and answer Ms. Quelling's questions. But she found herself writing things like *What if I still get a D because of my other tests?* so many times she almost wore down an entire eraser.

"Want one of my *new* pencils?" Anne-Stuart whispered.

"I'm fine," Sophie said.

"Sophie," Ms. Quelling said. "Look up the answers yourself."

But all Sophie could do was *pretend* to be reading. Even Antoinette could do no more than that.

The period dragged on until Sophie knew she would absolutely dissolve into a small puddle if Ms. Quelling didn't finish those reports in the next seven seconds.

And then suddenly Anne-Stuart whispered, "She's done!"

"You look scared," Julia said to Sophie.

Sophie didn't answer. She just watched as Ms. Quelling put a paper facedown in front of each student.

"If you've worked hard," Ms. Quelling said, "you have nothing to worry about."

No! Sophie wanted to cry out. *That's not true!*

Then Ms. Quelling put one at Sophie's place, and Sophie stared at its blank back.

What difference does it make? she thought. *Ms. Quelling hates me no matter what I do. I could get an A plus on my test, and she would probably still find a way to flunk me.*

Antoinette slumped in despair. With Henriette nowhere in sight, how could she find Lafayette here, trapped in the enemy camp? Where can I turn? she thought. And then it came to her, like a tiny candle flickering in the darkness. Go to the Master Jesus, it whispered. Imagine his presence. Antoinette raised her face to the light and closed her eyes. Behind her she heard a soft cough.

And then another, coming from Anne-Stuart. And still another, a louder one, from the back table, where B.J. was hacking into Kitty's sleeve.

"Do y'all need to go to the nurse's office?" Ms. Quelling said. "I'm going to start handing out cough drops at the door."

"You started it," Maggie said to Anne-Stuart, words thudding.

Both Julia and Anne-Stuart looked at her as if she were a passing worm, and then they focused on Sophie. She still hadn't turned hers over.

"The grade's on the other side," Maggie said.

"So—look at it," Anne-Stuart said. She crossed her fingers. "We're hoping for you."

Julia crossed her fingers on *both* hands and nodded toward the back of Sophie's paper.

Sophie wanted to fold it up and stick in her backpack and read it when there *weren't* three pairs of eyes watching her as if she were about to dive off a cliff.

But something stopped her. Maybe it was the crossed fingers and the nodding heads. Julia and Anne-Stuart could be rude sometimes, but who couldn't? Maybe they had some nice streaks in them, and maybe those were what were showing right now. Maybe they weren't more evil than good.

Slowly Sophie lifted the paper and looked at it. Julia and Anne-Stuart practically climbed across the table. Sophie saw the small B- in the space marked "This Week's Grade Average" and felt herself going limp.

"Is it bad?" Anne-Stuart said.

Sophie shook her head and turned it around. Julia's eyes scanned it and landed. Her smile stuck in place, but a storm seemed to pass over her face. Anne-Stuart gave Julia a stricken look.

Sophie pressed the paper to her chest. Neither of the Pops had said a word, but all traces of "We're hoping for you" were gone. She could only think one thing: *They were hoping all right—hoping I would fail.* An odd kind of nausea went up her throat. It had been one thing to be invisible to the Pops. But she was sure no one had ever *hoped* she would flunk. She shrank into Antoinette's cloak.

Maggie pointed at Sophie's paper. "What does the comment say?"

"I haven't read it," Sophie said.

"Well, look at it," Maggie said. "That's what *my* mother always goes for right away—the comment."

Sophie looked. *I'm seeing improvement*, Ms. Quelling had written, *but I suspect it hasn't happened honestly, though I have no proof at this time. Will watch the situation carefully. I have separated her from Fiona Bunting. Would advise that you do the same.*

"That isn't true," Maggie said over Sophie's shoulder. The bell rang. Sophie snatched up her backpack and charged for the door. Fiona was on her heels, and Sophie thrust the paper into her hands the minute they were in the hall.

"B minus!" Fiona said. "That's brilliant!"

"Read what she wrote, though!" Sophie said.

Fiona's eyes grew wider as they swept the page.

"No!" she said. Then she pushed the report back at Sophie and took out her own. "I haven't even read *my* comment," she said.

She pulled Sophie closer to her as they stared at Ms. Quelling's writing: *Fiona continues to do above average work. However, her recent association with Sophie LaCroix may hurt her. I suspect cheating and will continue to keep diligent watch. I trust you will take appropriate action regarding this new friendship.*

Fiona stuffed the paper into her pack like a wad of trash.

"That woman is beyond heinous," she said. "She's pure evil. And so are her little T.P.'s."

"T.P.'s?"

"Teacher's pets." Fiona's eyes went into little gray slits again. "Teacher's *Pops*."

Sophie felt a whisper of a smile on her lips. "You mean *Corn* Pops."

"They *are* Corn Pops!" Fiona let out a bitter laugh. "They're just corny and fake, but they think they're all that."

Sophie grinned. And then just as quickly, she felt the cloak fall on her, heavy and dark.

"What if our parents believe her?" she said.

Fiona shrugged. "Your parents know you're not a cheater." Fiona gave her a gentle push toward the computer room door.

"Let's get through this class so we can go play. I'm suffocating in this place."

The solid C in computers and Ms. Y's comment, *Good to see this*, didn't do much to lift Sophie's spirits. She was just surprised Ms. Y had managed to squeeze in a comment at all. Ms. Quelling had used up most of her space too, with her scissor-words.

Sophie said to Fiona when they were on the playground after lunch, "I'm sure Ms. Quelling hates me."

"It's not true."

They both looked down from the monkey bars. Maggie was squinting up at them, one sturdy hand shading her eyes like a salute.

"*What* isn't true?" Fiona said.

"That you cheated on the test in Ms. Quelling's class."

"No, it *isn't* true," Fiona said.

They both continued to look down at Maggie. Sophie didn't feel like talking to anyone except Fiona.

"Just so you know," Maggie said. "I know the truth."

She waited another few seconds, and then shrugged and walked away.

"I guess we weren't that nice to her," Sophie said. She threw her head down on her crossed arms. "I'm too depressed to even play."

In math Mrs. Utley gave Sophie a C- and wrote: *The grade is a gift for solid improvement. Expect to see more in the future.*

When she handed it to Sophie, Mrs. Utley said to both Fiona and Sophie, "Looks like you're having some problems in Ms. Quelling's class."

"It isn't true," Fiona said. "We don't cheat."

Mrs. Utley surveyed them from within the puffy folds around her eyes. "A little advice then?" she said. "Don't give anybody a reason to think you do cheat."

"Can I still help Sophie in this class?" Fiona said.

Mrs. Utley wiped her forehead with the side of her hand. "I'm going to let you, at least for the time being." And then to Sophie's surprise, she put her plump hand on Sophie's shoulder. "Just be sure you pay as much attention to *me* in class as you do to Fiona. Then maybe you won't need her help so much." She gave Sophie's shoulder a warm, damp squeeze. "You're a smart girl."

As the teacher moved slowly off to the next table, Kitty dropped a folded piece of paper in front of Sophie and skittered off.

"She's the Corn Pop errand girl," Fiona whispered. "Don't open it."

"What if it's an apology note?" Sophie whispered back.

"Are you insane?" Fiona said. Sophie slipped the note into her backpack. But she forgot about it the minute she climbed into the Suburban after school.

"How did your day turn out, Dream Girl?" Mama said. "Did you get your C's?"

Sophie nodded, although it was hard to even move her head.

"You don't seem very happy about it," Mama said. "This means you'll get your camera."

"Can I go to Dr. Peter today?" Sophie said.

"Not until tomorrow." Mama stopped at the stop sign and looked at Sophie. "All right now, you're scaring me. You look like you just lost your best friend."

"I think I'm going to!"

"Why?" Mama said. She pulled away from the stop sign.

Sophie took out the progress report and read Ms. Quelling's comment out loud. She could hear her voice trailing like a broken strand in a cobweb. Mama all but pulled over onto the side of the road.

"Sophie," she said. "What is going on? No, wait till we get home." Mama put her hand up and pressed the accelerator. She careened into the driveway like a NASCAR driver. Lacie bolted out the front door.

"Sophie's social studies teacher called," she said. "She wants you to bring Sophie straight back to the school—like NOW."

Nine

Sophie felt her heart slamming against her chest. *It's over*, she thought.

Everything is over. Mama didn't even get out of the car. "We have five minutes," she said to Sophie as the Suburban sent gravel flying. "So start talking."

As the neighborhood went by in a blur, Sophie told Mama everything. When they reached the school parking lot, Mama turned off the ignition and faced Sophie squarely across the seat.

"Look me in the eye," she said. "Did you and Fiona cheat?"

"No, ma'am," Sophie said.

"All right then," Mama said. "Let's get this mess straightened out."

Mama looked at least three inches taller as she marched up to the school. It made Sophie lift up her own chin and walk fast to keep up. Seeing Fiona in Ms. Quelling's room when they got there made her feel even stronger. Fiona was sitting calmly next to Boppa at a table, hands in her lap.

Boppa stood up until Mama had taken a seat. Ms. Quelling was nowhere around.

"Are you as fired up about this as I am?" Boppa murmured to Mama. He had a tiny red spot at the top of each cheekbone.

"I feel like a mother bear," Mama murmured back.

Fiona grabbed Sophie's hand under the table and held on.

It's all right, Antoinette tried to say with the squeeze of her hand. Not even a council of Loyalists can take us down. We are the patriots in this battle. And we have the Wise Ones to defend us. We are not alone.

The door from the hallway opened, and Ms. Quelling bustled in and opened her office door. Out came the train of Pops. Julia Cummings. Anne-Stuart Riggins. B.J. Schneider. Willoughby Wiley. Kitty Munford.

Fiona's hand gave Sophie's a clench that clearly said, *We're doomed.*

"May I ask who these ladies are?" Boppa said. He sounded proper, as if he were in a bank.

"These are the girls who informed me on Friday that Fiona and Sophie had a secret cheating code."

The Corn Pops all gazed innocently at Ms. Quelling. All but Kitty, who was swallowing as if she had an elephant stuck in her throat.

"And you believed them," Mama said.

"I listened to both sides," Ms. Quelling said.

"And you believed *them*," Mama said again.

Ms. Quelling wafted a hand over the Pops. "I've known all of them except Kitty since they were in kindergarten. They're nice girls." She cleared her throat. "However, I think it's possible that they were mistaken this time."

Julia's eyes startled, and she raised her hand halfway. "We aren't mistaken."

Anne-Stuart nodded. "We wouldn't have said anything if we weren't sure."

"I'm certain of that, girls. I just think someone else may have been privy to additional information." She tilted her chin toward the hall and called, "Come on in."

Maggie stepped in, stomping to the front like a chunky soldier.

"This is Maggie LaQuita," Ms. Quelling said to Mama and Boppa. "Maggie, please tell everyone what you told me."

"They didn't cheat," Maggie said. "Fiona and Sophie had a code of signals. But it isn't what you think. Fiona coughs at Sophie when she sees her daydreaming, so she can keep her mind on her work."

"How do you know that, Maggie?" Ms. Quelling said.

"I heard Sophie and Fiona talking about it all last week."

Julia raised an arm, ponytail swinging. "Maggie could be lying for them."

"I don't think so," Ms. Quelling said, her voice soft. "That's the same story Fiona and Sophie gave me Friday when I questioned them."

It sounded to Sophie as if Ms. Quelling were apologizing to the Pops.

"I'm sure you girls were just trying to help," Ms. Quelling said. "But next time, you might want to check out your facts a little better before you make an accusation, okay?"

"We never meant to make trouble," Julia said. Her friends all nodded except for Kitty, who put her face in her hands and cried.

"Did you want to say something, Kitty?" Ms. Quelling said.

"She's really sensitive," Anne-Stuart said. "She doesn't like to hurt anybody's feelings."

"None of us do," Julia said.

Fiona dug her nails so hard into Sophie's palm that Sophie was sure she was going to draw blood.

Ms. Quelling turned to the group at the table. "I'm sorry," she said. "I'm sure you can see why I was torn. I'll remove my comments from Sophie and Fiona's permanent records. Please accept my apologies."

"Apology accepted," Mama said without smiling. Boppa nodded in agreement. He didn't smile either.

"Can we go now?" Julia said.

"Yes. Thank you, girls," Ms. Quelling said.

The Corn Pops hurried through the door, and Maggie trailed out behind them. Fiona held onto Sophie for about fifteen seconds before they, too, escaped to the hall. By then, the Corn Pops were down at the other end, gathered in a circle around Kitty, who was wailing like a baby.

Maggie suddenly appeared and stood in front of Sophie and Fiona.

"Thanks for sticking up for us," Sophie said. "You saved our lives."

"Yeah, thanks," Fiona said. "Only from now on, could you not spy on us?"

"I won't have to anymore," Maggie said. "Because I'm going to be playing *with* you." She gave them a logical smile. "I figure now you owe me."

"Oh," Sophie said. "Well then, we'll see you tomorrow—at lunch, I guess."

As Maggie walked off in even, plodding steps, Fiona turned to Sophie, mouth already open in protest, but Boppa and Mama came out of Ms. Quelling's room.

"I'm sure you two want to spend some time with that camera tonight," Mama said. Her eyes were shiny. "Boppa says you can come over now and stay for supper, Fiona, if you both get your homework done first thing."

Fiona and Sophie squealed in unison.

After dinner, during which Sophie could barely take a bite of meatloaf, Daddy unrolled the progress report. He let his eyes work down to the bottom and rolled it back up. He tapped Sophie lightly on the head with it and gave her the Daddy-grin.

"Looks like I'm going to have to turn over that camera."

Sophie shrieked so loud she was sure she sounded like Willoughby.

Daddy showed them that the camera was pretty simple. The buttons he said she needed to know about seemed made for her as they fit in all their silvery-ness under her fingertips. The minute she squinted into the eyepiece it became *clear* that Sophie's world was meant to be seen through a camera lens. As she pointed it at Fiona, her friend filled a frame that shut out all the mundane stuff.

"Let's get started!" Fiona said to her. "Henriette and Antoinette are waiting!"

They worked until dark. When they viewed their first film on the camera's tiny screen, Antoinette and Henriette often had their heads chopped off, but Mama said it wasn't bad for a first try.

"We'll get better with practice," Fiona said.

"You think?" Sophie said.

"Oh, definitely. We can do this whole thing over tomorrow at recess."

Daddy looked up from the viewer. "You're talking about at school?"

"Yes," Fiona said. "We can do whatever we want after lunch for almost a half-hour."

"Sophie can't take the camera to school," Daddy said.

"Why?" Fiona said.

Sophie winced. Daddy looked startled that she had even asked, and his voice went into lecture mode. "One: it's expensive, and if it disappears, I can't replace it."

"My dad would just give you—"

"Two: I see nothing but trouble developing with those little—"

"Girls," Mama said quickly.

"—who can't mind their own business. And three: the whole idea of having this camera is to focus Sophie on her pretend stuff when it's appropriate. And that isn't at school."

Fiona watched him, bright-eyed. Daddy suddenly grinned at her. "Do you need more information?" he said.

"No, that's plenty," Fiona said.

"Why don't you two do your planning during free time and then do the actual filming after school and on weekends?" Mama said.

Fiona nodded. "We'll figure out a schedule." She looked at Sophie. "Do you have a planner on your computer?"

"I don't have my own computer," Sophie said.

Daddy groaned. "Don't put any ideas into her head, Fiona. The video camera about broke me."

"You're exaggerating," Mama said to him.

"He is the veritable master of hyperbole," Fiona said.

Mama and Daddy both stared at her.

"She has an excellent vocabulary," Sophie said.

"No kidding," Daddy said.

Even though the next morning was gray and misting, Sophie got up feeling lighter than she had since they had moved to Virginia. Fiona was waiting for her on the stage with two breakfast burritos, homemade by Marissa. Sophie smiled all through the morning. She even smiled at Anne-Stuart when she saw her in the hall outside Ms. Quelling's room.

Anne-Stuart sniffed at her. "Did you read my note from yesterday?"

"No," Sophie said.

Anne-Stuart whispered directly into her ear, "You should read it." She smiled in a wispy way and disappeared into the classroom.

"What did she say?" Fiona said. "Was it evil?"

"No," Sophie said. "She was being kind of nice."

Fiona narrowed her eyes. "Sophie, you trust people too much."

"I've just been thinking about it," Sophie said. "Julia said they weren't trying to get us in trouble. Maybe they thought they were doing the right thing."

"And maybe I'm Marie Antoinette and nobody knows it." Fiona leaned into Sophie. "Don't let them fool you. They're just manipulators. They turn things around any way they can to get what they want."

Sophie was quiet as she followed Fiona into the classroom. Why would the Corn Pops just decide they hated her and Fiona and want to get them into trouble? It didn't make any sense.

She reached inside her pack to get her textbook and remembered the note. She smoothed it out and she read Anne-Stuart's round, perfect handwriting, done in purple gel ink that smelled like grape bubble gum.

Dear Sophie,

I just want you and Fiona to know since your both new that me and Julia and B.J. have always been the top in our class. Just so you know what your deeling with.

Your friend,
Anne-Stuart

Sophie blinked when she got to the end of the note. *How did she get to the top of the class?* she thought. *She can't even spell, for one thing.* Still, Sophie felt stung. The Corn Pops had definitely *not* been trying to do the right thing.

She crumpled the note and stuffed it back into her pack, and she could almost feel the eyes boring into her from every direction. Sophie closed her eyes and imagined a quick glimpse of Jesus. He was smiling, kind as ever.

Okay, Sophie told herself. *As long as we're more good than evil, we'll always be all right.*

"Ms. Quelling—please!"

Sophie looked at B.J., who was leaning over Ms. Quelling's desk, raking her hand through her butter-blonde hair.

"If I do switch you with Maggie," Ms. Quelling said, "will you and Julia and Anne-Stuart yak your heads off?"

"No, ma'am," B.J. said. Sophie didn't see how B.J. could even talk with her lower lip hanging out that way.

"Why are you so hot on this, B.J.?" Ms. Quelling said.

B.J. squatted down and spoke so low, Sophie could barely hear her.

"I want to be moved away from Kitty," B.J. whispered.

Ms. Quelling nodded and gave Kitty a pointed look. "Fine," she said. "I'll switch you with Fiona."

"But I want— "

"How does it feel to want, B.J.? Work with me here."

Julia tossed her mane of auburn hair toward Anne-Stuart.

"It's okay," Anne-Stuart muttered to her. "At least she got away from Kitty."

Julia nodded. "We'll get us together again." She dug her eyes into Sophie.

Don't look at me, Sophie thought. *I didn't ask to sit here.*

As soon as they could get out of the cafeteria at lunchtime, Fiona and Sophie bolted for the playground. Fiona had her

Idea Book so they could plan how to redo their video. But no sooner had they settled themselves on the top bars than someone else climbed heavily up to join them.

"So what are we doing?" Maggie said.

Fiona pulled the Idea Book to her chest. "We?" she said.

"I get to play with you now, remember?"

"Oh, yeah," Fiona said.

Sophie's stomach churned. This was one kind of scene she didn't like—

Antoinette sighed and took Magdalena by the hands. "If you are to be one with us," she said kindly, "there are certain rules you must learn and follow. Can you do that?" Magdalena bent her head. "I would do anything to be a part of what you have with Henriette."

Sophie looked up sharply. Maggie was staring down at the hands that held hers. Sophie pulled her palms away. "You did practically save our lives. So—" She looked at Fiona. "Let's tell her our rules."

"You can't have rules," Maggie said. "There aren't any adults to enforce them. Can't we just get on with the movie? What about costumes?"

"We'll put them together," Fiona said. She was barely opening her mouth because her teeth were clenched together so tightly.

"You don't have to," Maggie said. "I have tons, and what I don't have my mom can make us. She's a professional tailor."

"Great," said Fiona. Her voice was as dull as Maggie's.

"You need me for something else too," Maggie said.

"What?" Fiona said between her teeth.

"Who's going to run the camera when you two are in a scene together?"

Fiona scratched at her nose. "You?"

"And who's going to play Lafayette?"

"You?" Sophie said.

Maggie shrugged. "So what are we waiting for? Let's get to work."

Ten

At free time on the playground and after school at Sophie's, the girls, including Maggie, practiced the rest of the week for Saturday filming. But there were problems.

In the hall after language arts class one day, B.J. "accidentally" ran into Sophie as she passed, shoving her into Fiona and landing both of them against the wall.

"Are you all right?" Anne-Stuart said. Fiona told Sophie later that Anne-Stuart's voice was laced with concern, but her eyes spelled pure contempt.

"What's contempt?" Sophie said.

"It's when somebody thinks they're better than you are," Fiona said. Fiona and Sophie weren't the only ones being tormented by the Corn Pops. Kitty Munford was now excluded from the Pops' lunch table.

But Kitty still trailed after them down the hall in spite of their curled-lip glares over their shoulders. She handed Julia and B.J. and Anne-Stuart notes, which they smelled and wrinkled their noses at and threw away. One day Sophie and Fiona even saw Kitty running after them on the playground wailing, "Why are you mad at me? Why don't you like me anymore?"

Julia finally stopped the whole group and turned around slowly to face Kitty.

"We're not mad," she said with a plastic smile. "We've just moved on."

Kitty covered her face with her hands and stood there sobbing as Julia led the Corn Pops away.

"That was just heinous," Sophie said to Fiona.

"But you know what's even worse?"

Sophie shook her head.

"Kitty still wants to be friends with them after the way they treat her. It's absolutely pathetic." Fiona pulled Sophie toward the monkey bars. "Come on. We have work to do."

And then, of course, there was Maggie. She was always armed with ideas she said were the *right* way to do things. It made Fiona talk with her teeth gritted.

But Maggie *was* teaching Sophie something new about the camera every day. Now when Sophie held it, her eye UNsquinted at the little window, she could turn it on with ease and zoom in or out on Lafayette or Henriette. She could imagine herself as a Hollywood director, hollering, "Cut!" and waving her arms to express how she wanted things done.

"Lafayette shouldn't just stand there," Fiona told Maggie one day when the three girls were practicing. "He was the commander of an *immense* army. He stood tall—"

"I thought you said he was short," Maggie said.

"But he could *look* tall," Fiona said through her teeth. "He was—*commanding*."

You should know how to do that, *Maggie*, Sophie thought. *You command* us *all the time*.

The train of Corn Pops passed by just then.

"Flakes," Julia said to her followers.

Fiona watched them go by with contempt in her eyes.

"Flakes?" she said. "From a bunch of Corn Pops?"

Sophie felt a smile whispering across her face.

"What's so funny?" Maggie said.

"Well," Sophie said, "if they're the Corn Pops, then I guess we must be the Corn *Flakes*!"

"No way!" Maggie said. "I don't want to be a Corn Flake!"

But Fiona looked at Sophie and gave her husky laugh. "I love that!" she said. She reached out her hands to give Sophie the secret handshake.

"What are you doing?" Maggie said.

Fiona and Sophie looked at each other.

"It's just a thing we do," Fiona said.

"So—I'm a Corn Flake. I need to learn it."

"I thought you said you didn't want to be one."

Maggie looked at them soberly. "Maybe I do," she said.

With everything going on, Sophie now had to take more and more Jesus-breaks just to sit and feel his kind warmth. *If you love me*, she would think to him, *how come you don't make people understand me and my fellow Flakes?* There was still no answer, not one she could hear anyway.

But by Friday after school, Sophie could think only about their movie. She had scored B's on all her tests except math, which was a C+, and they were completely set for filming. They had chosen a wooded area near Poquoson City Hall as their setting. Mama said they were absolutely not going into some isolated area by themselves and arranged to go with them. Lacie pitched a fit, because that meant Mama wouldn't be at her soccer game, and Sophie held her breath until Mama said, "Don't start with me, Lacie."

At last, the mistress was scolding the maid Lacette. Antoinette tried to feel smug, but as she looked at Lacette's crestfallen countenance, she couldn't help feeling sorry for her, in spite of everything.

On Saturday morning, Sophie was helping Mama unpack the Suburban at the edge of the woods when Fiona arrived.

"I have a surprise," Fiona said. She held up a metal contraption with three legs.

"What is it?" Sophie said.

"It's a tripod. Boppa made it for us. There's a place to screw our camera to it so it won't wobble around so much. You can still pan from side to side and up and down if you want to, but it won't be all shaking from you or Maggie holding it." Just then a horn blew, and a faded blue car the size of a small boat pulled up. Maggie emerged from the passenger seat and motioned Sophie and Fiona to help retrieve three bulging garbage bags from the backseat.

Mama went around to the driver's side and stuck her hand in the window.

"I'm Lynda LaCroix," she said. "You must be Maggie's mom."

"I'm Rosa," said the older version of Maggie. For Sophie, there was just enough of a trill to her R to make her voice romantic.

"Sophie!" Fiona said. "Look at all this *cool* stuff!"

Sophie turned to where Maggie was pulling clothing out of a bag. She held up a pale pink satin dress with flounces on the sleeves and a lace-up front.

"This is yours," Maggie said to her. "There's a cloak in here for you too. Mom made it your size."

Sophie took the dress and held it against her as Maggie pulled out a long, forest-green dress with matching cape for Fiona and a dashing white uniform with red trim, for her to wear as Lafayette.

"That's exactly how I imagined him!" Sophie said.

"We looked it up in a book," Maggie said. "If we're gonna do this, we want it to be real, right?"

"Now all we need is a musket for him," Fiona said. She was breathless.

"I brought one," Maggie said. "It's fake, of course."

It wouldn't have surprised Sophie if it had been the real thing. Everything else was so *exactly* the way the guides in Williamsburg dressed that Sophie had to keep blinking to make sure she wasn't still dreaming.

Out of the last bag Maggie began to pull a black cape—velour, not velvet, but with a hood big enough for all of Sophie's hair. Its plush fabric never seemed to stop unfolding.

"Oh, Maggie," Sophie said. "It's magnificent!"

"I knew you'd say that," Maggie said. She didn't smile, but her eyes, for a moment, looked soft.

Breathless, Sophie donned the luscious black cloak. The woods were ablaze with autumn leaves. There was just a hint of a chill in the air. From someplace close by, someone had a wood fire going, so its time-honored aroma drifted into their scene. It was magically 1779 in Williamsburg.

With serious faces, Fiona and Maggie set up the tripod and made ready for the first scene. From then on, Sophie *was* Antoinette—elegant and brave and held in honor by Henriette and the Marquis de Lafayette. And yet she was also Sophie Rae LaCroix, famous filmmaker, intent on making a fine film that would pack theaters everywhere.

There were a couple of problems though. Once, Sophie forgot to turn the camera on, and they had to do a whole scene over. The other thing: Maggie couldn't act.

"She's like a stick saying words," Fiona whispered to Sophie.

Sophie tried to coach her, but Maggie just stared with a blank face.

"I wish you spoke French," Fiona said.

"I could do it in Spanish," Maggie said.

"Do that," Sophie said "At least it's a foreign language."

It helped. When they were wrapping up the final scene, Fiona said she wished they could go back and do *all* of Maggie's scenes in Spanish. It was already two o'clock, and they had to dig into sandwiches in the Suburban while Mama drove everybody back to their house to be picked up.

"I have an idea," Mama said.

"Is it scathingly brilliant?" Fiona said.

"I think so. Why don't we have a premiere at our house tonight?"

"What's a premiere?" Maggie said.

"It's a first showing," Fiona told her. "People get all dressed up—can we do that?"

"Absolutely you can," Mama said. "Soph, get Daddy to help you burn the DVD. And I'll set up the family room and make some *hors d'oeuvres.*" Mama said they should invite their parents and come over about seven.

Sophie spent three hours getting ready, which was good because she wasn't allowed into the family room until Fiona arrived with Boppa.

"My parents already had plans," Fiona said. Her gray eyes were sparkling. "But your mom said I could sleep over."

When Maggie and her mom appeared, both with their hair up in fancy buns, Mama said, "Shall we go in?" She put out her hand to take Daddy's arm and led the way. Lacie wanted to know why she was wearing a long skirt just to go to the family room. Sophie swished her black cloak and wished Lacie would be whisked away by bats.

The family room was breathtaking, Sophie thought. Candles burning. Chairs set up like an intimate theatre. Computer-printed programs on each seat, announcing the premiere of *Antoinette and Henriette Save the Day for Lafayette.*

"This is fabulous," Mrs. LaQuita said.

"It's amazing," Daddy said. "My wife is terrified of the computer."

"You did a great job here," Boppa said.

Mama looked at Sophie and smiled her elfin smile. "It was worth it."

When the first scene finally wiggled its way onto the TV screen, Sophie was immediately lost in the delicious black cloak and the way it swirled when she walked. Lost in the drama of Antoinette begging Henriette not to die. She was even lost in the stiff-legged Lafayette, who looked into the camera when he was supposed to be professing his undying gratitude to Antoinette.

"Oops—there goes that fast pan again," Daddy said. He too seemed engrossed in their movie. "Who had the camera then?"

"That would be Sophie," Maggie said.

"You have to remember to move it very slowly, Soph," Daddy said. "Much slower than you would think. There are a couple of other things, but overall this isn't too bad."

"I think it's wonderful," Mama said. "Better than that thing we rented the other night."

Sophie wished everyone would simply watch the story. It was so beautiful she could hardly bear it. She could actually *see* what she had been dreaming of for so long, exactly the way she had imagined it. She had to put her hand to her chest so it wouldn't burst.

At the end, everyone clapped, and Boppa kissed each of the girls' hands. Maggie pulled hers away as if he had taken a bite out of it, but Sophie thought it was romantic. Everything was floating on a cloud—until Lacie ran out of the room choking and sputtering.

"She was laughing," Maggie said.

"What was your first clue?" Fiona said.

Sophie looked at Mama and Daddy, but neither of them went after Lacie to tell her how rude she was.

Let her laugh, Sophie thought. *Just wait until I become a famous movie director. Lacie won't scorn me then.* That *wasn't just a dream. It was really going to happen someday.*

Eleven

Late that night, with flashlights under the bedspread and the now dog-eared Idea Book, Fiona and Sophie got right to work on the sequel.

"You know something?" Fiona said. "Now that Lafayette has gone back to France, we don't really need him. We can write Maggie out."

"Wouldn't that be rude?"

Fiona pressed her mouth tight, and then she said, "I think she was the reason Lacie thought our movie was so lame. Maggie was always bossing us around. And then *she* couldn't act her way out of a wet paper bag. Wasn't it embarrassing to watch her play Lafayette?"

Sophie had to admit that it was. But she still had a squirmy feeling inside.

"We'll have to give back the costumes," she said.

"Oh, yeah—huh?"

"I really like that cloak."

"*You* make Antoinette what she is," Fiona said. "Not the cloak."

Sophie sighed. "We have to tell her in a nice way."

"I'm not as nice as you are," Fiona said. "You think of something."

Sophie closed her eyes. She imagined Jesus, although his eyes looked more sad than kind, and he wasn't smiling. When she imagined Antoinette, she was holding a feathered pen over a piece of parchment, but there were tears in her eyes.

"I think we should write her a farewell letter," Sophie said. "We should write like they did in the eighteenth century."

"Boppa has an actual inkwell—and those pens you dip in. He'll let us use that."

"Does Boppa say yes to everything?" Sophie said.

Fiona nodded. "He does it to make up for my parents, because they're never around." She tapped her Idea Book with her pen. "So—you dictate the letter to me, and then we can get all the stuff tomorrow and do the real one."

The letter Sophie came up with was, as Fiona called it, a masterpiece. It took them until longer than expected to get the eighteenth century version done, because Maggie showed up at Sophie's house Monday afternoon and wanted to know what the Corn Flakes were going to do next. They wouldn't be able to put the finishing touches on the letter until Tuesday, after Sophie's session with Dr. Peter.

"I don't see why you have to keep going to him," Fiona said. "You're doing so *good*! You're making B's now."

"I don't know," Sophie said. But she didn't really care.

The minute Sophie was curled up in Dr. Peter's window seat, she started right in. "Daddy still doesn't get me," she said.

"He's still after you about those daydreams, huh?"

Sophie hugged a face pillow to her chest. "It's better now that we're making them into movies. But it's still 'Sophie, do it this way.' Or worse, 'Sophie, why can't you be more like Lacie?' And he keeps reminding me that if I don't *keep* my grades up,

I can't use the camera. And I *have* to!" She tilted up her chin. "I'm going to be a film director someday. For real."

"I don't doubt it for a second," Dr. Peter said. "Would you like to try something fun with me?"

"Yes," Sophie said.

"I want you to pretend that you are *you*." He wrinkled his nose with a grin. "And I'll pretend to be your father. What's my name?"

"Daddy," Sophie said. "But couldn't it be like I'm Antoinette and you're my papa? Sometimes now when I don't know what to do, I imagine Antoinette, and then I know."

"Do you know why that is?" Dr. Peter said.

Sophie shook her head.

"Antoinette *is* you. She is the very strong and brave you. How do you think she got the way she is if *you* didn't make her up? She is the *you* who knows what to do."

"I don't get it."

"Let's try this and you be Sophie. Just say whatever Antoinette would say, and that'll be you."

"I'll try," Sophie said.

Dr. Peter sat up very tall on the seat and puffed out his chest.

"All right, Soph," he said in a deep voice. "Let's talk about those grades."

Sophie burst into giggles.

"Excuse me?" he said in a deep voice. "I'm not messing around here."

"You sound just like my father!" Sophie said.

"I *am* your father!"

"Okay." Sophie sat up straight on the pillows. "Father—oops—Daddy, I'm doing the very best work I can in school."

"Well, you're making B's now. But why can't you make A's? You're every bit as bright as your sister."

Sophie searched for Antoinette. "That may *be*—Daddy. But you know, don't you, that I'm not the least bit like Lacette."

Dr. Peter gave her Daddy's pinch between the eyebrows. "Who is Lacette?"

"Lacie! Daddy, we are not the same. And sometimes I feel as if, like, you want me to be her twin, and I'm not. I know I wasn't doing my best before, but now I am—and it's MY best."

Sophie realized that she was crying. She took off her salt-stained glasses. Dr. Peter handed her a Kleenex and waited for a moment.

"It's all right to cry," he said. "You're showing your true feelings, and that's what you need to do with your dad. Just the way you did it just now. You were very calm, very respectful."

Sophie shook her head. "He would still yell at me."

"How do you know that if you've never tried?" Dr. Peter wrinkled his nose. "You know what, Sophie? You have nothing to lose. You tell me he yells at you now, so what would be the difference? And he might not yell. He might be so surprised, he couldn't say anything at all."

Sophie giggled again. "Like *that's* ever going to happen. He can *always* say something. He's really smart."

"That's where you get your intelligence. And from your mom you get your creative side." He nodded. "God began a very good thing when he made you. I know he's very proud of you."

Sophie stiffened against the pillows. "I don't get that," she said.

"Get what?"

"If God—if Jesus loves me so much, then why doesn't he make people understand me?"

"Why don't you ask him? Are you still imagining him there with you?"

"Yes—but he doesn't ever *say* anything!"

"He's probably working in a different way. But I'll tell you something." Dr. Peter leaned forward like he was about to tell her a secret. Sophie found herself leaning in too. "You know how I said Antoinette knows what to do because she's in you?"

Sophie nodded.

"Jesus also shows you what to do because *he's* in you."

"He doesn't show me!"

"Sure he does." Dr. Peter laced his fingers around one knee. "I want you to try something else on your own—just for this week."

"I just have to try, right?" Sophie said.

"Yes, just try. Whenever you don't know what to do, instead of imagining Antoinette, I want you to imagine Jesus, just the way you've been doing. Ask him what to do." He grinned. "And then wait until you know that something is right, and then do it."

"Wait?" Sophie said. "What if one of the Corn Pops is in my face? I have to stop and imagine Jesus right then?"

Dr. Peter blinked. "You've lost me. Is this a new game—you being chased by cereal boxes?"

"Nooo!" Sophie explained the Corn Pops and the Corn Flakes to him.

"That's really clever," he said. "You know that, don't you?"

Sophie shrugged.

"Let me just say one thing about that, and then we have to finish up." He adjusted his glasses. "I think the names are great. Just be sure you look past the group's nickname. Be sure you look into each person. Especially when it comes to yourself."

"Okay," Sophie said.

"That's it for today then."

He high-fived her, and she was off to finish the letter with Fiona. When they were finished, there was only one tiny blob of ink on the paper, which Sophie thought made it more realistic. Still, when she and Fiona put it on Maggie's table first period on Wednesday, scrolled and tied with a ribbon, Sophie had a hard time letting go of it.

"It's going to hurt her feelings," Sophie said.

"Would you rather have her there bossing us around?" Fiona edged away from the table. "It just isn't the same with her there. I liked it better when it was just you and me."

Sophie at once felt sorry for Fiona—more sorry than she felt for Maggie. She left the parchment scroll on the table, and she forced herself not to look at Maggie the whole period. In social studies, Maggie wouldn't look at *her.*

"I think we worked it out," Fiona said after lunch. They were sitting on a set of swings no other sixth-grader would be caught dead on.

"I guess," Sophie said. "Did she read it? I didn't see her read it at all."

"I think we're about to find out." Fiona sat up straight. "Here she comes."

When Maggie reached the swings, Fiona said cheerfully, "Hi, Maggie."

"I didn't come to say hi," Maggie said. "I came to say that you didn't have to go to so much trouble because I thought the movie was stupid anyway." She gave her dark hair a flip with her hand. "And who *wants* to be a Corn Flake?" Then she turned and walked back toward the school building.

"She thinks she's 'all that,'" Fiona said.

Sophie pulled a strand of hair under her nose. "I don't want to talk about it right now." She closed her eyes and imagined Jesus. He was as kind as ever. She felt worse.

What do I do? Sophie said to him. *I don't think what we just did was right—but I don't know what to do. If I call Maggie back,*

Fiona will be mad at me. She probably won't want to be my friend anymore.

She waited, just as Dr. Peter had told her to, but there was no sudden burst of inspiration. There was only Fiona saying, "Come on—that was the bell."

Sophie climbed off the swing, but Fiona stayed on hers.

"Soph?" she said. "Are you mad at me?"

"No!" Sophie said.

They gave each other weak smiles and walked back to the building together.

But for the rest of the day, Sophie felt more alone than she had in a long time. The office lady bringing her a note last period from Mama didn't even help: *Your mother is going to be about ten minutes late picking you up. She wants you to wait on the playground, and she will find you.*

"They must have told her in the office that's the safest place to be after school," Fiona said. "There's always a teacher out there." Fiona tilted her head almost shyly. "I wish I could stay with you."

Sophie said she wished she could too, but secretly she was glad to be alone as she headed for the swings. She needed to badger Jesus until he showed her something. Sophie pulled up her sweatshirt hood. The thought of her lost black cloak stabbed her.

"Jesus?" she whispered. "Did we do the wrong thing, kicking Maggie out?"

There was a scream—though Sophie knew right away that it wasn't Jesus answering her. It was coming from across the playground, where a small group was streaming away from the fence, leaving behind a lone figure who was waving her hands and screaming. It was Kitty.

The group walking away from her was the Corn Pops. Not a single one of them looked back.

Sophie took off toward Kitty, but Julia planted her tall self right in Sophie's path.

"Don't go there," Julia hissed. "Just leave it alone, or you are going to be so sorry."

Twelve

Julia kept looking at Sophie through hardened eyes — until Willoughby gave a stifled squeal and B.J. pulled at Julia's elbow.

"Mr. Denton is coming!" she said in a hoarse whisper.

"Just leave it alone," Julia said to Sophie one more time. Then she was gone, with her train of Pops behind her.

Do they really think Mr. Denton isn't going to see Kitty over there freaking out? Sophie thought.

"Everything all right out here?" Mr. Denton called.

"Yes!" Kitty called back. "I'm fine!"

Mr. Denton waved and sat down on a bench by the door. Sophie hurried over to Kitty and squatted down beside her.

"Why did you tell him you're fine?" Sophie whispered to her. "What did they do to you?"

Kitty's face was smudged with dirt on both cheeks, except where tears had left their trails on the way down her face.

"Please don't tell anybody," she whispered. "Please."

"But *why*?"

"Because!" Kitty rubbed her eyes with the backs of her hands, leaving them smeared with dirt.

Sophie grabbed one of Kitty's dirty hands. "What happened?"

"You have to promise you won't tell anybody else—and you can't tell Julia and them that I told you either."

Kitty hung her head until all Sophie could see was the top of her ponytail. "I had to crawl on the ground. They told me that if I crawled across the playground on my hands and knees, they would take me back into their group."

"What?"

"And then after I did it, they laughed and said they were only joking. They never wanted me back in their group at all!"

Kitty shook her head so hard, Sophie was afraid she was going to break her neck.

"Stop!" Sophie said. "They aren't even worth it! They're just—cruel. They're evil—they're heinous!"

A whistle echoed across the playground. Sophie whirled around—but it was only Mr. Denton. Mama was standing next to him with Zeke, waving at her.

"I'm coming!" Sophie called to her. She turned back to Kitty.

"Please don't tell anybody," Kitty said. Her eyes were pleading. "If you do, they'll find out about it—they know *everything*—and they'll do worse to me."

Sophie didn't know what to say, and Dr. Peter had told her to wait if she didn't know.

When she got home, Sophie went straight to her room. Her stomach was tying itself into a knot as she sat cross-legged on the bed.

"Jesus?" she whispered. "I saw two people get really hurt today. I think I have to do something about it. I'm just going to ask you what to do, and then I'm going to wait until I know. Because somebody has to do something. And I think it's supposed to be me. Is that why I'm feeling so sick?" She swallowed hard. "Or is it because I was hurting somebody else myself?"

Sophie kept her eyes closed and waited. Just as always, there was no answer she could hear from Jesus. She wiped her wet face. "It's *wrong*," she whispered.

After she somehow got through dinner, Sophie called Fiona.

"There's something we have to do," Sophie said when she had Fiona on the line. "But you have to promise not to tell a single other person, or Kitty is going down."

"Kitty?" Fiona said. "Do we care about Kitty?"

"Yes," Sophie said. "We do."

Sophie told Fiona everything she had witnessed on the playground.

"So what are you saying we should do?" said Fiona.

"I think we should rescue Kitty."

"What?"

"And I thought about something else," Sophie said. "What the Corn Pops did to Kitty is no different from what we did to Maggie."

"It wasn't like we just stopped being her friends! We were *never* her friends!" Fiona's voice was winding up. "She pushed herself right on us. She was making us pay her back for something she did for us, and we paid her back. We're done."

"I just don't like the way we did it," Sophie said.

"It was *your* idea!"

"I know. And that's why I think we should tell her why we got mad at her and give her one more chance."

"No," Fiona said. "And you know what else? I'm not helping Kitty either. Has she ever once been nice to us?"

"I don't think that makes any difference," Sophie said. "We should do the right thing."

"*You* do the 'right thing,'" Fiona said. "Not me!"

Suddenly there was a click in Sophie's ear. Fiona had hung up.

Sophie flung the phone onto its cradle and climbed the stairs in a blur. But when she tossed her glasses onto the bedside table and threw herself face down on her bed, her chest was pulled in so tightly she couldn't cry. She could only lie there with hurt all around her until a knock sounded at her door.

"It's seven thirty," Daddy said. "You only have an hour and a half before lights out. Did you get your homework done?"

She really wished he would go away. She was afraid she was going to either throw up or cry, and she would have to explain either one. Dr. Peter had told her Daddy might understand if she just talked to him calmly—but now just wasn't the time to try that.

"I'm about to, Daddy."

"Okay. Well, let's get it done." Daddy opened the door a crack. "You want to keep that camera, right?"

Sophie nodded.

"Now that you're on track, I want to see some steady improvement. Let's make that the rule starting next week."

He ran his hand over her hair and left, whistling. Sophie felt as if a steamroller had just knocked her down. She couldn't do her homework. She couldn't even think about how she was going to rescue Kitty all by herself, or even how she was going to apologize to Maggie.

All she could think about was never being friends with Fiona again. Never having lunch together, never meeting on the stage behind the curtains with homemade breakfast burritos, never hanging out on the monkey bars and planning brilliant films.

She finally snapped off the light and crawled under the covers. *Is everything going to go back to the way it was before*

Fiona? she asked Jesus. *If you love me, why would you let that happen? Help me get her back, please.*

Just one more thing, she said to the kind-eyed man in her mind. *I won't crawl in the dirt for Fiona, okay? Please don't let her ask me to do that.*

And then she started to cry.

The next morning, being-scared nausea swept over Sophie as she walked through the school hallway alone.

What am I supposed to do now? she thought. *Fiona isn't waiting for me backstage. I can't go there by myself.* She put her hand to her mouth. *I wouldn't be able to bear it!*

Instead, she turned toward the language arts room. Maybe Mr. Denton would let her come inside and sit. Although what she was going to do or think about or dream up, even she couldn't imagine.

Sophie hadn't taken more than two steps when a skinny figure was beside her, sniffling.

"You've been crying," Anne-Stuart said in her clogged-up voice.

Sophie tried to ignore her and set her sights on Mr. Denton's door.

"Is it about Fiona?" she said. "She's been crying too. Julia's trying to help."

Anne-Stuart pointed a shiny-nailed finger. Sophie nearly tripped on the carpet. Fiona was against the wall, across from the language arts room, and Willoughby and B.J. stood in front of her, leaning in as if Fiona were giving them the ultimate secret to popularity. But it was Julia who astounded Sophie the most. She was standing next to Fiona—*with her arm around her.* And Fiona wasn't even flinching.

Thirteen

Sophie pushed open Mr. Denton's door and made her way to her table. She sank down into her chair, her backpack thudding the floor beside her. She put her head on her arms and tried to let Antoinette take over and push away the heinous sight of Fiona joining the Corn Pops.

Antoinette sat down beside her and pulled the black velvet cloak around both of them. "I'm so sorry, my gentle friend," she said, "but I am not your answer. The good doctor, the brilliant *doctor—he gave you the answer. You must follow that now."*

Sophie squeezed her eyes tighter. *You're leaving me too, Antoinette? NO—come back!* But Antoinette didn't, and Sophie felt more alone than she ever had. Maybe if she called Mama and told her she was really in trouble, they could go to Dr. Peter right this minute. He could tell her what to do. And then Sophie knew something: he already had told her what to do. With her eyes squeezed shut against the hot tears, she prayed.

The kind face was there in her mind—the Jesus face she always imagined. Not Antoinette's face. Not Fiona's face. Just Jesus'. And he had already shown her what to do. *If I have to do it on my own—then please will you help me?*

The bell rang, jangling her face up from her arms. The room filled with jabbering students followed by a substitute teacher. Sophie couldn't look to see whether Fiona would sit with the Corn Pops. Instead, she looked for Maggie.

I have to tell her I'm sorry, Sophie thought. She didn't know anything else at the moment, but she knew that.

As Sophie watched, Maggie settled herself into a corner and opened a book. Sophie glanced around and realized that on the board the sub had written: *THIS IS A FREE READING DAY.*

This is my chance, Sophie thought. *But what if I apologize and Maggie just yells at me?* And then she could almost hear Dr. Peter in her head: *She gets in your face anyway. What have you got to lose if you talk calmly and honestly to her? You'll never know unless you try.* Sophie wove her way through people who *weren't* reading. Maggie slammed her book shut just as Sophie sat down next to her.

"Hi," Sophie said. "What are you reading?"

"What do you care?" Maggie said.

Sophie squeezed her hands together. "I do care. Fiona and me, we made a huge—an *immense*—mistake when we wrote you that heinous letter. I hope you'll forgive me."

"Are you ever for real?" Maggie said. "Or is everything a big act to you?"

"This *is* real," Sophie said. "We thought you were *way* bossy when we were making our film, and we didn't like it. But we should have told you the truth." She had to stop and take a deep breath. "I want you to be a Corn Flake again, and I'll even help you remember not to be pushy. We can do the secret handshake—and we have a very important film to do. This one— "

But she stopped, because Maggie was shaking her head.

"Why not?" Sophie said.

"Because you just want the costumes," Maggie said. "My mother thinks you just used me, and she said if I start being friends with you again she'll ground me. Face it: Fiona dumped you and joined the Corn Pops, so now you need a friend." Maggie opened her book again. "It isn't going to be me," she said, and then she glued her eyes to the page and shut Sophie out.

But not before Sophie saw the title on the cover: *The Story of the Marquis de Lafayette.*

She wants to be friends—I know she does, Sophie thought as she moved back to her table, her feet like a pair of concrete buckets. *But we hurt her feelings so bad that even her mom hates us now.*

Suddenly Sophie knew something else too. Once you hurt somebody, you have to take the consequences. She looked over at Kitty, her literature book open and her eyes wistfully watching the people who had made her crawl across the playground like a dog.

I want the Corn Pops to know that too, Sophie thought. *I have to find a way. Even if I have to do it alone.*

As soon as she could at lunchtime, Sophie fled from the building. She couldn't bear to go to the monkey bars. *It's bad enough that Fiona doesn't want to be with me*, she thought miserably. *But I never, ever thought she would be a Corn Pop.*

But she had a mission. Sophie plopped into a swing and pored over her social studies book to find out what Lafayette and George Washington had done in their rescue of America. It wasn't *exactly* the same thing, although she found some inspiring ideas—like the patriots digging trenches called "redoubts" to hide in and trapping the British "handsomely in a pudding bag."

Sophie closed her eyes several times and imagined Jesus when the planning got too lonely. He was always looking at her with kind eyes, but sad ones too—as if he understood that even though what she was doing was right, he knew it wasn't fun for her without Fiona. *I'll just have to go back to pretending on this plan*, Sophie said to him in a prayer. Daddy wouldn't like it, but she couldn't help thinking Jesus did.

This plan just might work. It had to.

After school, Sophie couldn't wait to get to Dr. Peter's window seat.

"Sophie-lophie-loodle!" he sang out. "I can tell you've got something on your mind today." Dr. Peter was barely seated before she was pouring out the whole Maggie and Kitty and Fiona story. Dr. Peter listened and nodded. There was no twinkle at all.

"Can I just tell you how proud I am of you?" he said.

"I feel wretched," Sophie said.

"Well, look at you. You went to Jesus. You asked what to do. You waited. He showed you—and you did it."

Sophie shook her head.

"No?" Dr. Peter said.

"Yes. But I'm still not sure *how* he showed me. I want to know in case he does it again."

Dr. Peter spread out his fingers and counted on them as he talked. "Showing number one: you never go out on the playground after school, but the day you did, there were the Corn Pops giving Kitty the worst time ever. Didn't that turn you around completely?"

Sophie nodded.

Dr. Peter started on another finger. "Your prayer showed you later that you had to get with Fiona and apologize to Maggie.

None of that has worked out the way you want—yet. But you did the right thing. And besides that—" His eyes twinkled as he went to finger number three. "You had a substitute so you could talk to Maggie."

"But what *about* Maggie?" Sophie said. "She still hates me."

"I think Maggie is still choosing. Otherwise, why the continued interest in Lafayette? Just because *you* take the opportunity Jesus gives you doesn't mean everybody does. You can't decide for another person. You can only give them the chance."

"So—let me get this straight," she said.

"Okay." Dr. Peter wiggled all his fingers, telling her to bring it on.

"When Jesus 'shows' me something, it isn't like *boom*—there it is! It's more like he gives me an opportunity, and then I decide whether to take it or not."

"Exactly," Dr. Peter said. "That's how it works."

Sophie tickled her nose with her hair. "But what I still don't get is, if Jesus loves me so much—"

"Okay, there's your hang-up," Dr. Peter said.

"Where?"

"That 'if.' When you say '*If* God loves me—*if* Jesus loves me,' that means you have some doubt. As long as you have that 'if,' you're going to doubt the opportunities that Jesus puts right in front of you. I'm sure that bums him out." Dr. Peter leaned forward. "God loves you. There is no 'if,' Loodle. That's why he sent Jesus to show us the way—he loves you *that* much. He's our Father—and you know how much a father loves his kids."

Sophie looked down at the ends of her hair.

"What?" Dr. Peter said. "You don't think your father loves you?"

"I know he loves me," Sophie said. "But I don't think he loves me *that* way."

"Tell me some more."

"He would love me more if I did even better in school," she said slowly. "And if I played sports and joined all these clubs. I do think he loves me more than he did when we moved here. But it's never going to be enough, because— "

Dr. Peter's voice went down to an almost whisper. "Why, Sophie?"

Sophie squeezed her eyes shut tight. "Can I tell you something I've never told anybody else in the entire galaxy?"

"If you want to."

"I think my father loves Lacie more than he loves me."

"Sophie," Dr. Peter said, "do you remember when I told you that I would never tell anyone anything you said in here without asking your permission?"

Sophie nodded.

"I'm asking permission now to share this with your father."

"But he'll get mad at me!"

Dr. Peter smiled at her. "We'll never know that, will we, unless we try." Dr. Peter said there was one more thing.

"The key to everything is knowing that God loves you, and he shows you that love through Jesus. If you really want to believe that, you need to get to know Jesus better—not just in your imagination, but from who he is." He rubbed his hands together. "How did you learn more about Lafayette so you could start a good Kitty Rescue Plan?"

"From our social studies book," Sophie said.

"Okay—God has a book too."

"The Bible."

"Brilliant! Next time, we'll start reading the Bible and getting to know Jesus' plans too. But for now, you just focus on your plan to rescue Kitty." He stood up and grinned at her.

"I know this is hard, Sophie-lophie, but you go for it. I'm so proud of you."

That—and her talks to Jesus—carried Sophie through another evening without a phone call from Fiona. In fact, the next morning as she stepped inside the school building, she was ready for Scene One.

Kitty sat on a bench, looking painfully alone, staring at the literature book that Sophie could tell she wasn't reading. On the other side of the hall, the Corn Pops were standing in front of the trophy case, comparing new sweaters with their backs very deliberately to Kitty. At least Fiona wasn't with them.

Sophie headed straight for Kitty. "Come with me, would you?" she whispered to her.

Getting her away was like peeling a sticker off a mirror, but Sophie managed to drag her through the double doors and into the hall in front of the office where nobody hung out. By then Kitty was barely breathing.

"You didn't tell anybody, did you?" she said. "I told you not to tell!"

"It's not about that," Sophie said. "I just want to tell *you* something." She took Kitty's hand, Antoinette-style. "Those girls out there—you don't need them. They're mean to you."

Kitty whimpered. "I know. But I'm so mixed up!"

"Why?"

Kitty pulled in air that sounded ragged. "I knew they could be sort of mean. Like when they got jealous of you and Fiona doing good in class, they *looked* for ways to get you in trouble. Like they swore you made up the coughing code so you could cheat, even though they didn't know for sure. I got really scared then about saying stuff about people that wasn't exactly true, and that's when they decided to dump me." Kitty shuddered. "Then I saw how mean they can *really* be, and I just want them to leave me alone now. Only— " She put her hand over her mouth and mumbled into it. "I just don't want to be all by myself."

"You don't have to be alone," Sophie said. "They're not the only girls in the galaxy. You can be my friend."

Kitty looked at her, and then darted her eyes away. "No offense," she said. "You're really nice, but I want to be with the popular girls. I was way popular at my last school. Now I don't know if I'll ever be popular again."

"You don't have to be popular to have fun," Sophie said. "I have a *lot* of fun when I'm with—well, I have fun."

Kitty didn't look at her this time. "But everybody thinks you—and Fiona—are weird." She burst into tears. "I don't want to be weird!"

Sophie knew that at this point Fiona would be telling Kitty that *she* was the one who was weird. Sophie actually considered it too, but instead she said, "There are four other girls in our class besides us and the Pops— "

"They're the soccer players. I can't— "

"Okay. Well," Sophie said, "if you ever decide you don't mind being with weird people, come see me, and I'll be your friend. But in the meantime, I can still help stop Julia and those other girls from being mean to you. It won't make them be friends with you, but at least they'll leave you alone."

Kitty shook her ponytail sadly. "Nobody can stop them, because everybody thinks they're wonderful. I told you, even the teachers wouldn't believe me."

"They would if they *saw* them being mean to you."

"Unh-uh. They never do anything mean when teachers are watching."

"Leave that to me," Sophie said. "Just come out to the playground after school."

"But that's when they do mean stuff to me!" Kitty said. "They know the teacher on duty doesn't get out there until way after the bell."

"Trust me," Sophie said. "Please. All you have to do is, when they start to do something to you, *run* over to where I'm playing. They'll follow you, and I'll do the rest. Mr. Denton will have seen what he needs to see already. I promise you."

"I don't know," Kitty said. "I can't even stand it when they *start* with me!"

Kitty bolted for the girls' restroom. Sophie watched her for a minute and then trudged the hall to the language arts room. She could almost hear Dr. Peter saying, "You've given her an opportunity. Now it's her choice."

Fourteen

Scene Two didn't go the way Sophie hoped it would either. She went up to Mr. Denton at the end of language arts and asked him if he could come out to the playground *right* after school.

"As soon as the bell rings, if that's feasible," she said.

"Actually, I'm not on duty today," he said. He folded his arms and smiled, something he didn't do very often. "Too bad too. You've got me intrigued."

Sophie squinted her eyes. "Who *is* on duty today? Mrs. Utley?"

Mr. Denton shook his head. "Ms. Quelling is the victim today."

"Oh," Sophie said.

She could feel herself wilting as she turned away.

"Something I can help you with?"

Sophie looked at Mr. Denton in surprise. He was giving her a kind look. That was why she said, "Do you pray?"

"I've been known to," he said.

"Then please pray for me today. I need it."

"You are a fascinating child, Sophie LaCroix," Mr. Denton said. "You have my prayers."

Sophie felt a little better after that, especially as Scene Three of the plan unfolded. Out on the playground after lunch, she was able to dig a trench—her "redoubt."

I think the actual ditches the soldiers dug were deeper than this, Sophie thought as she worked. But she really didn't want anybody to break a leg. She disguised the trench with some branches and then gave a big sigh. This would have been brilliant with Fiona. There would have been so much more to it—they were such a good team.

"*Were*," Sophie said to herself.

Before she could start crying, she headed back toward the school building. Near the back door, the Corn Pops were all gathered, watching Anne-Stuart French braid Julia's hair. Fiona was nowhere to be seen. They stopped their conversation and put on identical freeze-dried smiles as Sophie started to pass.

"Hey," Julia said.

Sophie had to look twice to realize Julia was talking to her.

"Hey," Sophie said back. She edged toward the door.

"Are you trying to be friends with Kitty now?" Julia said.

Sophie took a deep breath. Fiona always handled this kind of stuff.

"Does it matter to you?" Sophie said. "You're not friends with her anymore."

"No," Anne-Stuart said. "But—well—" She looked at the rest of the Corn Pops, and they all nodded as if they already knew what she was going to say. "I don't mean to be talking bad about Kitty," she went on, "but she whines *all* the time. She always makes everything look worse than it is because she *cries* so much."

"I wonder why?" Sophie said. She knew that her pipsqueak voice didn't make her sound sarcastic the way Fiona could.

"So," Julia said, "are you going to be friends with Kitty now?"

"If she wants to be," Sophie said. "I asked her to come out and play with me today after school."

"Really?" Anne-Stuart said. "Is she coming?"

Sophie didn't answer. She was too busy asking Jesus to forgive her if she was pulling Kitty into a trap. But this had to be part of the plan—and the Corn Pops had just made it so easy.

Julia patted her newly braided hair. "It's nice to know she'll have someone to *play* with, since we don't *play*." She lowered her voice as if to include Sophie in a little-known fact. "Just be careful. She really is a whiner."

"Yeah," Willoughby said, in her usual whine. "We hate that."

Scene Three closed as the bell rang, and Sophie waited until the Corn Pops were inside before she fell into the line filing through the door.

I think they'll be there, she thought. *Because they don't want Kitty to have* any *friends. Or me either.* It gave her a chill that went all the way to her backbone.

Kitty was hanging just inside the door when Sophie got there. Her freckled face was a tangle of confusion.

"I saw you talking to them," she whispered to Sophie.

"I was setting it up," Sophie whispered back. "You have to just trust me."

As Sophie continued down the hall, she heard Kitty whimper.

I wouldn't blame her if she never trusted anybody ever again, Sophie thought.

Just as soon as the bell rang at the end of the school day, Sophie went into high gear to get ready for Scene Four.

She raced to the bathroom and got into costume. The old bedspread from the attic wasn't one tenth as wonderful as the cloak Maggie's mother had made for her, but Sophie decided she would just have to be a better actress to make it work—although it was going to be hard enough doing the scene all by herself.

It doesn't have to be good, she told herself. *It just has to do the job.*

She looked at her somewhat ragged self in the mirror. *I'm Antoinette, and I'm tattered from this long war. But I'm ready to face the British so the final battle can begin!*

When she got to her spot by the fence, Sophie cleared off the branches and lay down on the ground, looking over the top of the redoubt. All she could do now was wait for Kitty and the Corn Pops—and hope Ms. Quelling had shown up for duty.

Why does it have to be her and not Mr. Denton? she thought.

And then she had to smile to herself. If this worked, who better to see it all than Ms. Quelling, who thought the Corn Pops were perfect?

A rustling sound behind her interrupted Sophie's thoughts. Sophie rose up to see, and then she flattened herself again. The Corn Pops were arriving from the other direction.

"Are you ready, Antoinette?" she whispered to herself.

Her heart pounding, Sophie got up and began to deliver her lines down into the trench in a stage-loud voice.

"Don't fret, Private! I've bandaged your wound! It should hold until this final battle is over!"

It was pretty convincing, Sophie knew. She definitely wanted to make the Corn Pops think she wasn't aware they were there. But she couldn't hear them over her own voice. That was one thing she hadn't thought of. She knew Fiona would have.

Sophie shook her head under her mobcap and went into pantomime. Beyond her, Kitty's voice was fragile, but loud—and upset—enough to hear.

"Just leave me alone!" she cried.

"We just want to talk to you," B.J. said. "Come here!"

"We're going to give you one more chance." It was Anne-Stuart this time.

"No!" Kitty said. "You'll just play a trick on me!"

Their voices were getting closer. Sophie's heart pounded harder, but she just pantomimed in bigger gestures. It wasn't time to make her move yet.

Julia's voice rose over Kitty's, silky and smooth. "We don't play tricks. Sometimes we joke around—private jokes. You're just too sensitive."

"I just don't know when you're joking. It seems mean to me."

Uh-oh, Sophie thought. It sounded like Kitty might be giving in.

"We're not joking right now," Julia said. Her voice was like pancake syrup.

"In fact," Anne-Stuart said, "we're all going to swear a friendship oath and we want you to do it too."

By now it was obvious that they had stopped moving. *Don't listen to them, Kitty!* Sophie wanted to call to her. She bit down on her lip and pretended to watch anxiously for Lafayette over the horizon. She was careful not to look straight at the group.

"Why do you need an oath?" Kitty said.

"Well," Julia said. "Some people have been telling our group's secrets."

Sophie recognized Anne-Stuart's sniffle. "You know, like about our private jokes."

"We don't know who it is," Julia went on, "so we're *all* going to swear an oath."

"We're not going to cut ourselves or anything," B.J. said.

"Gro-oss!" Sophie was sure that was Willoughby.

"Then *what*, Julia?" Kitty said.

"We are all going to cut our hair *really* short."

"No, you're not!"

"Yes, we are," said Anne-Stuart. "We'll all help each other do it."

"I don't think I want to do that. I look awful with short hair!"

"Kitty!" Julia's voice almost sounded genuinely hurt. "Do you think I would make you look ugly? We're all still going to be cute."

"You'll be adorable," Anne-Stuart said. "And everybody else will start wearing theirs the same way."

Sophie heard the *snap snapping* of something metal.

"I've got the scissors," B.J. said. "They're exactly the kind stylists use."

"If you don't trust me, Kitty—" Julia sounded as if she were purring, "I guess I'll understand. You can do your own then. I'll hold your ponytail for you, and you can just—"

"No!"

Sophie went down on one knee. Kitty was coming closer again, and fast, and Sophie didn't want to mess things up now.

"If you can't take the oath with the rest of us," Julia said, "then maybe you're the one who told our secrets to somebody."

Her voice was coming closer too, but Sophie kept on acting and didn't look.

"Nooo!" Kitty said, closer still.

"Then what's the problem?" Anne-Stuart said. She was obviously right on Kitty's heels.

"Here, you want the scissors?" B.J. said.

There was an awful pause.

"Give them to me then," Julia said.

"Nooo!"

That's it, Sophie thought.

And then it was no longer just a plan. It was real, and it was happening.

Sophie sprang up, sweeping her bedspread cloak out to her sides, and shrieked "Kitty! Over here!"

Kitty ran the few steps it took to get to her, and Sophie folded her into the cloak and pushed the whole bundle behind her.

The Corn Pops were running too fast to stop. All four of them stumbled over the redoubt. Julia sprawled headlong, scissors flying from her hand.

Sophie scooped them up and held them over her head.

"Forfeit your recognizance, Redcoats!" she shouted. "We have got you handsomely in a pudding bag!"

B.J. still managed to say, "What?"

"You've been evil to Kitty for the last time," Sophie told them. She could feel Kitty shivering against her back, still cocooned inside the bedspread. "I *know* your secret. Your power is lost. The war is *over*!"

"What's going on over here?"

Sophie had never been so glad to see a teacher, even if it was Ms. Quelling.

"She's trying to attack us with scissors!" Julia cried. She pointed up at Sophie, who was still holding them up out of reach.

"Don't even try it, Julia," Sophie said. Her voice sounded like somebody else's, coming out of her own mouth. "She saw you go after Kitty with them."

"I didn't see anything except these girls all huddled together like they always are," Ms. Quelling said.

"You didn't see them threatening to cut off all of Kitty's hair?" Sophie said.

"No—where *is* Kitty?"

Sophie slowly stepped aside, her heart diving for the pit of her stomach. Kitty clung to her like a baby koala.

"I was trying to protect her," Sophie said.

"From whom?"

"From them!" Sophie pointed with the scissors at the Corn Pops.

"Let me have those before somebody puts an eye out," Ms. Quelling said.

Sophie handed them over and then put both arms around Kitty so she herself wouldn't shake.

"Thank you, Ms. Quelling," Anne-Stuart said breathlessly. She reached down to help Julia up and deposited her into B.J.'s waiting arms. "We were so scared."

"We were just playing around," Julia said, "and all of a sudden, Sophia was all grabbing at Kitty and waving those scissors around, saying she was going to cut *our* hair off."

Ms. Quelling looked at Sophie. "Is that true?" she said.

The only thing that kept Sophie from retreating back to Antoinette-land was the fact that Ms. Quelling actually looked surprised.

"No, it isn't true," Sophie said.

"Yes, it is," Julia said.

Kitty whimpered.

"Don't worry," Sophie said to her.

"You promised me," Kitty said. And then she really started to cry.

"You know we wouldn't hurt anybody, Ms. Quelling," Julia said. "You've known us since we were in kindergarten." She looked at Sophie and then at Kitty. "I don't mean to be rude, but both of them just moved here in the last six months. We don't know anything about *them*."

"Don't start talking like a York County aristocrat," Ms. Quelling said. "I don't think I can stomach it. At any rate, that doesn't prove a thing." She looked at everybody. "I can smell the fear in Kitty. She's so frightened of somebody that she's probably terrified to tell me which of you it is."

Sophie stole a glance at the Corn Pops. They were all open-mouthed, as if they couldn't believe Ms. Quelling wasn't hauling Sophie off to the office that very second.

"You know what really gets me?" Ms. Quelling said instead. "What really gets me is that any one of you would resort to behave this way toward people who are supposed to be your friends. You are intimidating AND manipulating. Teachers are always complaining about the boys who bully—but at least we can *see* what they're doing. Your business is secretive, and it's nasty—and it's deplorable. Do you know what that means, girls?"

Sophie was pretty sure she knew. It was heinous.

"I wish I did have proof," Ms. Quelling said, "because I suppose that's the only way we can put a stop to this—by making an example of someone."

"I have proof," said a voice.

It was a voice Sophie would have known even if she hadn't seen the wonderful gray eyes and the hair hanging over one eye. Fiona dropped neatly over the fence and walked past Sophie and Kitty, straight to Ms. Quelling. She was holding something behind her back.

"You were hiding and spying on us?" B.J. said. "That's not fair!"

"Yes, I was spying," Fiona said. "And how is that any more not fair than you trying to get Kitty to cut her hair just so you could humiliate her *again*?" Fiona looked at Ms. Quelling. "That's what happened. I saw the whole thing."

"You can't believe her," Anne-Stuart said. She was whining worse than Willoughby. "She's Sophie's best friend."

"Yeah, and you can't trust her," B.J. said. "She hung out with us all day all pretending to want to be our friend—and now we find out it was just so she could listen to our plans."

"Shut *up*!" Julia and Anne-Stuart shouted at her.

Ms. Quelling put both hands up and turned to Fiona. "Can you assure me that you are telling the truth?"

"I can do better than that," Fiona said. "I can prove it to you."

From behind her back, she pulled what Sophie now saw was a video camera.

"I've got it all right here," Fiona said. "Want to watch it?"

It really was over after that. By the time they had all watched the mini-screen in the principal's office, the Corn Pops were all bawling their eyes out. Principal Olinghouse dismissed Kitty, Sophie, and Fiona.

Out in the hallway, Kitty stood alone like a red-eyed baby bird.

"So—do I get to be a Corn Flake?" she said. "I don't care if it does mean I have to be weird."

Sophie gave her an Antoinette smile. "You can be anything you want when you're a Corn Flake. That's the beauty of it."

"Do I have to swear an oath or anything?"

"No," Sophie said. "You just have to let your imagination run free. You can imagine anything."

Kitty gave a nervous-sounding giggle. "I guess I could try. I've gotta go, okay?" She skittered down the hall and disappeared through the double doors.

"What about me?"

Sophie turned to look at Fiona. For the first time, she realized Fiona had tears smeared on her face.

"What about me?" Fiona said again. "Can I be a Corn Flake again?"

Sophie swallowed hard. "Do you want to be?" she said.

"I do—but only if you want me." Fiona shoved aside the strand of hair that was sticking to her wet cheek. "I knew I did wrong, like the minute I hung up on you. Boppa came into my room and found me crying, and I told him what happened, and *he* told me I should apologize to you and make it right, only—I was just afraid you wouldn't take me back. So I hung out with the Corn Pops to find out what was going to happen—so I could prove to you—"

"That you're still my best friend?" Sophie said.

Fiona's face crumpled. All she could do was nod.

"And I'm yours," Sophie said. "That's all I care about, Henriette."

"Me too, Antoinette."

Then they hugged and did the secret handshake. And then they promised to share it with Kitty the first chance they got, since she obviously needed the Corn Flakes as much as they did.

By the time Fiona left school in the SUV and Sophie went to call Mama, she was very tired—maybe too tired for everything that was still ahead of her, even after this victory.

There would be Daddy's reaction to Dr. Peter's talk with him. That probably wasn't going to be fun. And then explaining all of this to Mama and Daddy—and maybe hearing Daddy say Sophie had gone too far.

Plus trying to adjust to having Kitty and her spacey-ness around. *And* figuring out how to stop Maggie from hating them.

Antoinette reached out her hand and smiled from within the folds of her black velvet hood. "Why don't you go to Jesus?" she said. "He'll show you—"

And so, of course, Sophie did. And there was no need for anyone to cough him away.

Glossary

amie {AH-mee} French word that means "female friend"

contempt {kuhn-TEMPT} the act of being hateful

countenance {KOWN-tuhn-nuhnce} old-fashioned word that means face or facial expression; usually means your mood can be seen on your face

deplorable {dih-PLORE-uh-buhl} so bad that has to be fixed or changed

feasible {FEE-zuh-buhl} can be done; is doable

heinous {HAY-nuhss} unbelievably mean and cruel, or beyond rude

hors d'oeuvres {or-DURVS} French words that aren't pronounced the French way, but it means fancy little snacks

immense {IH-mentz} great or big, or enormously huge

imperious {ihm-PEER-ee-uhss} snooty, like someone who thinks he or she is better than everybody else

intimidating {ihn-TIH-muh-date-ing} making somebody scared with threats or making someone feel like he or she isn't as good as you are

intrigued {ihn-TREEGD} very interested in something; really curious

ma {mah} French word that means "my"

manipulating {muh-NIP-you-late-ing} when someone is turning things around to get what he or she wants, often in a sneaky, unfair, or not truthful way

manipulator {muh-NIP-you-later} somebody who is manipulating

mundane {muhn-DAYN} ordinary, commonplace, bo-orrring

pantomime {PANT-uh-mime} the art of telling or acting out a story without speaking, using just body movements instead

pathetic {puh-THEH-tick} really pitiful, or kind of sad

pessimistic {PEH-suh-MISS-tick} really negative or letting gloomy thoughts take over good thoughts; always seeing the bad side

privy {PRIH-vee} when somebody knows a secret

recognizance {rih-CAHG-nuh-zuntz} promising to appear in court; the court says it trusts you will come back. If you forfeit it (disobey), you have to pay a bunch of money.

serviette {serve-YET} French word that means "napkin"

thoracic {thuh-RAA-sick} of, about, or inside the thorax, which is the part of your body between your neck and stomach; it's like your chest cavity where your heart and lungs are